Last Seen in ██████████

By Anna Clarke

Last Seen in London

ANNA CLARKE

PUBLISHED FOR THE CRIME CLUB BY
DOUBLEDAY & COMPANY, INC.
GARDEN CITY, NEW YORK
1987

All of the characters in this book
are fictitious, and any resemblance
to actual persons, living or dead,
is purely coincidental.

Library of Congress Cataloging-in-Publication Data

Clarke, Anna, 1919–
Last seen in London.

I. Title.
PR6053.L3248L28   1987   823'.914   86-24396
ISBN 0-385-23559-3

Last Seen in London

CHAPTER 1

"Choose whatever essay topic you like," said Dr. Paula Glenning, lecturer in English literature at the Princess Elizabeth College of the University of London. "I don't care whether you like D. H. Lawrence or whether you loathe him, so long as you bring evidence to back up your statements. Okay, Cathy? Any problems?"

The little group of post-graduate students moved out of the room, arguing and laughing. Only the American girl remained behind.

"Did you want to speak to me?" asked Paula, glancing at her watch. "I'm not trying to hurry you away, but we'll have to vacate this room in a few minutes. You know I share it with James Goff, and he'll be wanting it for his seminar at half-past four."

"It's a lovely room," said the girl, looking around her at the high moulded ceiling and the long windows, perfectly proportioned, with their little ornamental iron balconies and the view of the lawns and plane trees of Prince Regent Square.

"Yes," said Paula. "The college took over this eighteenth-century terrace several years ago, and they've had the sense to keep the houses in their original form instead of knocking them down or pulling them about, which is what has happened to so much of Bloomsbury. I'm lucky to be here instead of in the main building, even if it does mean the inconvenience of sharing an office."

She paused and glanced at the girl, expecting her now to say something about what was troubling her. Cathy Bradshaw remained silent, standing near the door and clutching her little bundle of books and papers in a way that suggested tension and a troubled mind.

She was an exceptionally pretty girl, with a mass of black curly hair, deep blue eyes, and a lovely complexion. An Irish-type beauty, thought Paula, and wondered whether Cathy's ancestors had come from that country.

"Shall we go round to college and have some tea in the refectory?" she suggested. "It'll be noisy there, but maybe we can find a quiet corner to talk."

"Actually I did want to ask you something," said Cathy. "So if you could spare the time, Dr. Glenning . . ."

"Paula, please."

"Paula. I'm living right here in Prince Regent Square. The other side, in Bloomsbury Lodge. It's quiet there. Please, may I invite you to have tea with me?"

The invitation was given in a quaintly old-fashioned manner and with a studied British accent.

"Indeed you may. I shall be delighted to accept, Miss Bradshaw," said Paula with gentle mockery, but the moment she had spoken she regretted it, because Cathy looked both puzzled and hurt.

"Don't you invite people to tea in England? I thought you did."

"Of course we do," said Paula warmly. "All the time. I'd love to come, Cathy. And please forgive me. When one spends so much time with young people, one tends to develop a sort of defensive attitude of pretending never to take anything very seriously. Come on. We'll walk through the gardens."

In the flower-beds there were a few late roses in bloom, and the bright green grass was spattered with fallen plane leaves, golden brown in the October sunshine.

"It's just as I pictured it," said Cathy, lingering near a little maple tree, which bore a plaque stating that it was planted at the time of the Queen's Silver Jubilee. "Just what I've longed to see. Ever since I can remember, it's been my dream to come to London."

Paula was intrigued. She had taught many students from overseas, and most of them had been keen to come to London, but Cathy's emotion was of a quite different quality. She was touching the little tree trunk, almost caressing it, and then, as if regretting her outburst, she quickly walked on.

Cars were parked, illegally, so close together at the other side of the square that the women had difficulty squeezing between them, but the roadway in front of Bloomsbury Lodge was clear.

Paula knew the place quite well. It had been endowed by an association of scholars of all nations, and comprised three Georgian terrace houses converted into a residential club. The big rooms on the ground floor were used as dining-room, lounge, and meeting-room, and the bedrooms were on the three floors above. In the basement were the kitchen, various service rooms, and a self-contained apartment for the warden. In spite of the attraction of free accommodation in the heart of London, the Committee of Management always had difficulty in getting suitable people to do the job.

Bloomsbury Lodge was something of an anachronism, as Paula's informant had told her. Young students and visiting scholars nowadays much preferred to cater for themselves rather than to have meals at stated times; and the sort of academic gracious living that the founders had had in mind was impossible on a very limited budget. There remained a certain charm in the shabby elegance of the public rooms, but towards the top of the building the accommodation became more and more dilapidated. Bathrooms were draughty, drains got blocked up, beds were hard and lumpy, lamps and electric fittings sometimes downright dangerous.

Keeping the place in working order at all had defeated a succession of wardens, and the present incumbents, Joe and Marjorie Gainsborough, had more or less given up trying to maintain the furniture and fittings of the building and were concentrating on providing good food and an easy-going atmosphere.

The policy seemed to work, at any rate as far as attracting residents was concerned, and the rents were very low.

"As I didn't know anybody in London, I thought it would be best to be in a dormitory. I mean a hostel," added Cathy, hastily correcting herself.

To the left of the front door was a rather fine old mahogany desk on which stood a small telephone switchboard, a vase of chrysanthemums, and various books and papers. Behind it sat a dark young man reading a massive-looking volume entitled, so Paula managed to make out from where she stood, *Elements of Economics for Students of Sociology.*

He looked up as they approached, gave Paula a brief, appraising glance which said plainly that she didn't interest him, and then turned to Paula's companion and said, "Hi, Cathy," in a proprietary manner.

"Hullo, Carlos," said Cathy politely, in what Paula was beginning to think of as her "British" manner. "This is my tutor. May I bring her to tea?"

"Sure. Help yourself. It's in the lounge."

"Thank you. Come on, Paula."

From the door of the lounge Paula glanced back to the enquiry desk and saw the boy staring after them with a look of bewilderment on his expressive face.

The residents' lounge overlooked backyards and the backs of houses in the next street. It was a finely proportioned room and full of comfortable old armchairs, but Paula, who loved light and air, found it rather gloomy and claustrophobic. The tea, however, which Cathy poured from a large metal teapot covered with a woollen tea-cosy, was hot and fresh, and there were cucumber sandwiches and a coffee-and-nut cake.

"You wouldn't get this in a hotel," said Paula appreciatively. "It's like the first scene of *The Importance of Being Earnest.*"

Cathy smiled at last, a delightful smile, which took from her face the rather sombre expression that it wore when not in movement and gave her an air of innocence and vulnerability.

For a few moments they ate and drank in friendly silence, and then Joe Gainsborough came into the lounge, ostensibly to replace a copy of *The Times* on the table where the newspapers lay, but really, Paula suspected, to see who was there.

He walked past an elderly Japanese woman who was frowning over a map of Central London spread out on her knees, and came towards the window.

"Paula Glenning it is. If I'd known you were coming—"

"Cathy and I are continuing our seminar," said Paula, hoping Joe would take the hint and leave them alone.

He was a fair, stocky man in his mid-forties, dressed like a student and over-anxious to give a youthful impression. Paula had only a slight acquaintance with the Gainsboroughs, but whereas she had friendly feelings towards Marjorie, who always looked worried and overworked, she found Joe both irritating and pathetic.

Cathy was no help. She seemed to have withdrawn into a private world of her own, leaving Paula to do the talking.

Paula praised the tea and enquired after Marjorie and, because she felt guilty about disliking Joe, was more encouraging than she had intended to be.

At last Joe said, "I must leave you ladies. Duty calls."

He looked around. The Japanese woman was still struggling with her map. He walked over to her and made a show of being helpful before he left the room.

"I don't believe he's got any duties," murmured Cathy, coming out of her trance. "He's bone idle. Mrs. Gainsborough does all the work, and she teaches night school, too."

"Joe does some Open University tutoring," said Paula, "and he's written a couple of textbooks that are still used and need revising from time to time."

Cathy didn't look very convinced by this not very enthusiastic defence of Joe, and Paula, struck by an idea, went on to ask whether he was being a nuisance.

"Sexually? No," replied Cathy. "But he does find a lot of excuses for being up in my room. Mending the cold water faucet—I mean the tap—but it drips as much as ever. Or fixing a lock on the window. It doesn't work either. But that's not what's worrying me."

Cathy looked across at the Japanese woman, who was now folding up her map, and did not speak again until the door of the lounge had closed behind her.

"Paula, I'm scared. Right here in Bloomsbury Lodge."

It was said almost apologetically and with that sudden smile that made her look so young.

"Not by Joe Gainsborough?"

Cathy shook her head. "I guess I can handle him if need be."

"The reception clerk—Carlos?"

"Oh no. He's no problem."

Paula was a little surprised at Cathy's confidence, but told herself that, not being in possession of exceptional good looks, she could not know the sense of power and security that they would bring.

But surely danger, too?

"It sounds so silly," Cathy went on, "that I hardly know how to tell you. Do you remember Brontë's description in *Villette*, of the old woman who creeps about the school with a candle in the middle of the night?"

"Madame Beck," said Paula. "Yes, she's a sinister old girl. Don't tell me you've got one like that in Bloomsbury Lodge!"

She spoke lightly, but to herself she was saying, This is just the place for some eccentric old scholar to hide away, going quietly, or not so quietly, mad on one of the upper floors.

"Tell me more," she said. "Is somebody pestering you, Cathy?"

"I don't know whether you could call it pestering." The girl spoke slowly, as if she was now regretting having spoken at all.

Paula waited.

"Honestly, it's so darned silly that I'm ashamed to tell you, but it's worrying me, and I'd like an independent opinion. I'd very much like somebody else to tell me what they think of her."

Her, thought Paula. Definitely not man problems.

"My room's right up at the top," Cathy went on, "on the attic floor. There are just the two bedrooms with a landing between them and a bathroom. I had it all to myself until the day before yesterday, because the other room was unoccupied. It was rather nice. Like having my own apartment. Then this old woman turned up."

"What is she like?" asked Paula, as Cathy seemed to have fallen into a brooding silence.

"She limps a bit. She's slightly sort of . . . twisted."

Paula could feel the girl's revulsion as she spoke, the shrinking of the sound and healthy from the maimed and crippled in those first few moments before compassion took over from fear.

"I know what you're thinking," Cathy said, looking closely at Paula. "I'm not usually like this. Truly I'm not. I've got a young cousin back home who was born deaf. I've taught school where he lives. I've trained in speech therapy. I know what it's like to be alienated and disabled and not like other people. Please don't think I'm uncaring. Please don't."

The girl seemed close to tears. Paula reassured her, and she went on.

"Two nights ago there was a knock on my door at about ten o'clock, and when I opened it there was this woman standing there. She had very dark hair—it might have been dyed—and beady eyes, and she was dressed in black and grey and she was sort of twisted, like I said, and short—at least six inches shorter than me, with her head pushing forward and a smile on one side. She was like a spider, and I've got a horror of spiders. A phobia. I can't even stand to think of them."

Paula formed a vivid mental picture of Cathy opening the door of her attic room and expecting to see somebody like herself, or to see one of the Indian girls asking to borrow a kettle or a hairdryer, or even to see one of the Gainsboroughs, or the night porter on his security round, and seeing instead this spider-like woman.

"What did your visitor want?" she asked.

"To be of use to me. So she said. She came in and looked at my things—I was rearranging my clothes closet—and after she'd been touching my clothes I felt as if I never wanted to wear them again. There was something so . . . so greedy about her. As if . . . as if she wanted to possess everything. And yet I suppose she was harmless. Do you think I'm quite crazy?"

Again Paula received a strong impression of the scene in the attic room. "You were obviously frightened," she said. "I wonder why."

"I don't really know. She didn't actually do anything except admire my clothes," admitted Cathy. "She sounded quite normal and spoke with an English accent. Just ordinary. Not Cockney or anything. And not particularly high-class, as far as I could judge. She said she would be staying here for several weeks and hoped we would become better acquainted. She said she was looking up some facts in the British Museum for somebody who was writing a book about nineteenth-century London, but I didn't think that was true because she didn't look like anybody's research assistant. I guess it was just an excuse to ask about my studies and my life back home and the reason why I was here. I said as little as I could. She made me so uneasy."

"I suppose it could be true," said Paula, "that she was reading in the British Museum. You do find some very eccentric elderly people there. Some of them are a lot more odd than your old lady. It sounds as if she feels rather lonely in London and just wants somebody to talk to."

"I suppose so," said Cathy without conviction.

Paula felt rather at a loss. For a girl who had so firmly stated that she was well able to look after herself, Cathy was reacting very strongly to the nuisance of an unwanted acquaintance. Could it be that she was not so independent and self-assured as she wanted to appear? A spider phobia. Well, that was not so very uncommon. Certainly this old woman seemed to have touched off some deep spring of anxiety in her.

"Have you spoken to her again?" Paula asked.

"Yes. We keep meeting on the landing. She's doing it on purpose. She's lying in wait for me, and when she hears me on the stairs she comes out of her room. You heard how the stairs creak in this building. It's even worse up at the top. It's impossible to get up there without her hearing. I'm almost scared to come out to go to the bathroom."

"But this is absurd," said Paula. "What possible harm can she do to you? Have you told Mrs. Gainsborough?"

"I told you I was ashamed," said Cathy. "No, I haven't told Mrs. Gainsborough."

"Nor anybody else?"

"I asked Carlos if he knew anything about her, and he said her name was Mrs. Merton and as far as he knew she'd never stayed at Bloomsbury Lodge before."

"Mrs. Merton. Did that mean anything to you?"

"No," said Cathy, perhaps rather too quickly, Paula thought.

"Does anyone else know her?"

"Nobody I've spoken to. I did mention her to a nice old guy I've sat next to at meals. He's working at the British Museum, too. I think he's okay."

"And what did he say?"

"That if it's worrying me so much, why don't I change my room."

"Well, why don't you?"

"I don't think there are any others available," said Cathy evasively.

"What about other accommodation, then? I know it's cheap and convenient to be in Bloomsbury Lodge, but if it's upsetting you so much, I could probably help you to find somewhere else. There's a couple in our seminar—Leon and Victoria—who are looking for some more people to share the house they're renting near Regent's Park. I'm sure you'd be welcome there."

"Thanks," said Cathy. "It sounds fine. But I'd rather stay in Bloomsbury Lodge. I particularly wanted to come here."

"Why?" asked Paula bluntly.

"Because . . ." Cathy looked away. "I just want to stay here," she muttered after a moment's pause.

Paula rose to her feet. "Many thanks for the tea. I'd like to help you, Cathy, but if you only tell me half the story and then turn down every suggestion and won't let me tell Mrs. Gainsborough . . ."

She broke off. The girl was looking so hopeless and wretched that Paula controlled her little spurt of irritation and continued in a more kindly manner.

"What do you want me to do, then? If I can possibly do it, I will."

"I suppose you couldn't possibly come up with me now and see her for yourself? I'd like to have someone else's opinion, someone quite unconnected with it, before . . ."

Before what? Paula asked herself as Cathy suddenly stopped talking.

"All right," she said aloud. "Let's go up."

"This is a good time," said Cathy as they left the room. "She usually comes in about now. I'm awfully grateful to you. If you could just tell me what you think of her."

The lift was out of order, as happened so often, and it was a long climb to the top of the house. The elegantly curving staircase of the lower floors gave way to steeper, narrower steps, and the last flight of all, leading up to the two attic bedrooms, was uncarpeted and not, in Paula's opinion, at all suitable for a lame elderly woman to negotiate. Had Mrs. Merton chosen to be up here because the rooms were isolated, or because they were cheaper than the others? Paula determined to get hold of Marjorie Gainsborough at the first opportunity to find out, for her own satisfaction, what she could about Mrs. Merton.

"There's no sign of her," Paula whispered as they reached the top and Cathy turned left along the narrow landing.

"She won't come out if she knows I'm not alone," was the muted reply. "You see how I have to go right past her door and past the bathroom to get to my room. It makes me feel so trapped."

Paula did see, and was beginning to understand something of Cathy's problem. She was not herself of a nervous temperament, but she would have found it unpleasant to live up here in such close proximity to somebody she wanted to avoid.

"What about fire exits?" she asked as Cathy unlocked the door of her room. "That's what would worry me if I were here."

"You're supposed to get out on the roof. Look."

Paula joined her at the dormer window. Immediately below, there were a couple of feet of sloping tiles and then a narrow strip of flat roof, bounded by a low parapet, which appeared to run the whole length of the line of houses.

Paula looked down, and then from side to side, and made a face. "I suppose in an emergency, and with the flames at your heels . . . But you'd need to have a good head for heights. You'd be able to do it, and I could if I had to. But for elderly people . . . I must say I'm shocked that there's no proper fire escape. This looks terribly make-shift. I don't know how they get away with it."

"The whole place is terribly makeshift," said Cathy, "but I love the view."

It was a clear evening, and the light of day was giving way to the pink glow of the London sky. In front of them were the upper branches of a great plane tree, still plentifully hung with green and yellow leaves, and beyond were glimpses of grey sloping roofs, chimney-pots and television aerials, with the new high buildings down towards the Strand and the City forming a distant background.

"It's true. It's my dream come true," murmured Cathy, gazing out of the window as if she had found the treasure at the end of the rainbow.

Paula drew back for a moment, trying to recall moments in her own life when she had been similarly moved. There was her first visit to Paris, standing up on the hill in front of Sacré-Coeur and surveying the city. And St. Peter's Square in Rome—almost too overwhelming for delight. And yes, of course, much more relevant to Cathy Bradshaw, the Statue of Liberty, seen from the ship coming home from New York. That was a moment crowded with emotions.

She tried to enter into Cathy's feelings, but still she remained puzzled. Why should Cathy go into ecstasies over what was to Paula a pleasant but not exceptional London view?

Cathy's next remark went some way towards answering this question.

"You see," she said, smiling at Paula, "my father was English, and I've always felt that until I'd been to London I'd be only half myself."

Paula expressed interest and expected some further confidences, but Cathy seemed to regret having spoken, came away from the window, and asked Paula what she thought of the room.

"Hardly luxurious," said Paula, "but I've no right to give an opinion. My own apartment in Hampstead is rather like this. I'm always being told that I ought to move to somewhere larger and more comfortable, but I'm happy there and it feels like home. You must come and visit me. We usually have a get-together of post-graduate students before Christmas."

"Thanks. I'd like that. I ought to have said long before how much I'm enjoying the course."

Paula made a suitable reply, but it was evident that Cathy's mind was not on her studies.

"What shall we do now?" said Paula at last. "It doesn't look as if your old lady is going to appear. Shall we go and knock on her door?"

"She must be in the bathroom," said Cathy, looking worried. "But I haven't heard anything. It sounds like Niagara Falls when you use the bathroom."

"It's the same in my place," said Paula. "That's English plumbing for you. Anyway, I'd like to use the bathroom myself if I may."

"I'll get you some soap and a towel."

Paula took them and went outside onto the landing. A moment later she was back.

"It seems to be occupied. The door doesn't open."

"I don't understand it." Cathy sounded more and more worried. "I'm sure we'd have heard if she were there."

Paula suggested that they should go and knock, and Cathy, rather reluctantly, Paula thought, followed her.

The bathroom door, like those of the bedrooms, was ill-fitting and badly needed a fresh coat of white paint. As Paula had already discovered, the worn wooden door-handle was loose and did not grip, and the door seemed to be secured only by the little gadget just above it, which indicated VACANT and ENGAGED like the lock of a public lavatory cubicle. At the moment it appeared to have been pushed into a position somewhere between the extremes, since the letters ANT were visible, then a space, then the letters ENGA, but the bolt was near enough to the latter to hold in place.

Paula knocked and called out, "Is anybody in there?"

There was no response.

"She's got to be in there," said Paula, beginning to feel worried as well as puzzled. "Perhaps she's had an accident. I think we ought to fetch somebody, Cathy."

"Just a moment."

Cathy ran back into her room and returned with a pair of nail scissors. "I've had to do this before," she said. "If you bang the door hard enough the bolt slips of its own accord and you can't push it open. Whoever fixed this had no idea how to do the job. I could do it better myself. Look."

Paula looked. It was indeed a very awkward and flimsy piece of work, even by Bloomsbury Lodge standards. Not only was the bolt too loosely attached to the door, but the fitting did not fill the gap in the wood into which it had been inserted. Underneath it was a slit wide enough for Cathy to insert the points of the scissors and to get enough grip on the bolt to shift it along to the VACANT position.

She did this very neatly and competently. She was obviously a girl who was good with her hands.

"It's high time," commented Paula, "that somebody did some proper repair work on this building. I knew they were short of money, but it wouldn't take much to put a little thing like this right. I'm surprised at the Gainsboroughs. I thought better of Marjorie, at any rate."

Cathy completed her operation. The practical activity seemed to have eased the tension in her, but now that there was no further obstacle she hesitated and appeared reluctant to move.

Paula felt some reluctance, too.

"If I were living here," she said, "I'd push something up against the door when I was having a bath."

"I do. I push the chair up. But she hasn't done it now. The light's on, though," added Cathy, opening the bathroom door a little way.

Paula was conscious of a rather unpleasant smell of dampness and airlessness, and also of a sound like a dripping tap. There flashed into her mind Cathy's words—"She was sort of twisted . . . like a spider"—and partly to spare Cathy, partly to allow herself no time to be overwhelmed by Cathy's apprehension, she pushed forward in front of the girl and came into the bathroom first.

"Is she there?" called Cathy.

For a moment or two Paula was not sure.

The bathroom, like the two bedrooms, was built into the roof space, but it had no window and the lighting came from a single electric light bulb near the door. On the inside of the door was fixed a mirror, cracked and stained, and Paula was conscious of her own blurred and distorted image as she moved forward.

The bath was a relic of the Edwardian era, standing high up from the floor and with a broad curved rim, over which water was now gently spilling. Both taps were open a little way, and the overflow outlet could not quite cope with the steady incoming trickle.

At the very second when she stretched out a hand to turn off the taps, Paula saw the woman in the bath. Black hair spread out under the water like the strands of some monstrous sea anemone, encircling a little wrinkled face. Mercifully, the eyes were closed. Covering the body, like a shroud, was a long white nightgown.

"Is she dead?" asked Cathy in a low but steady voice.

"I think so," replied Paula, trying to remember what she had learnt in her first-aid classes, "but I suppose we'd better try to revive her. I'll take her feet."

Together they lifted the woman out of the bath. The girl was amazingly calm, and much more efficient at resuscitation than Paula.

Did she have any suspicion that this was what we were going to find? Paula could not help wondering as they worked together. *And was I meant to help her to discover it?* Cathy's exaggerated fear of the old woman, her refusal to consider leaving Bloomsbury Lodge, and all that business with the ramshackle door-bolt that could be manipulated from outside—all this added up to something of a mystery concerning not only the old woman but also Cathy herself.

Paula tried to get a grip on her racing thoughts. This must be an accident. An accident or a suicide. It was inconceivable that this highly recommended American post-graduate student could have known anything about it. Cathy had a spider phobia and Mrs. Merton reminded her of a spider. That was all. She barely knew the woman.

Or did she?

The questions continued to form themselves in Paula's mind. Whatever proved to be the cause of Mrs. Merton's death, one thing was certain: Cathy was not telling everything she knew. But she has brought me into this, decided Paula, and if she wants me to help her, then she has got to tell the whole truth.

"I don't think she's going to come round," said Cathy, sitting back on her heels and wiping her face with the back of her hand.

"Neither do I." Paula got to her feet. "But we had to try. Will you go and fetch somebody?"

They moved out onto the landing. The outside world, even the rest of the house, seemed a very long way away.

Cathy hesitated. It could be that she was tired from her labours; it could be that she wanted to be left here on her own. To remove some evidence, Paula asked herself, before anybody in authority came on the scene?

"Mrs. Gainsborough would be best," said Paula, "but if you can't find her, then tell her husband. Or the reception clerk. They'll have to telephone the police."

"The police?" The voice sounded alarmed again, the deep blue eyes looked startled.

"Of course," said Paula a little impatiently. "Don't let's waste any more time."

After Cathy had gone, Paula went back into the bathroom, keeping her eyes averted from what was lying on the floor, not because there was anything horrific about it but because it was so pitiful, so lacking in human dignity.

Had she got into the bath of her own free will? Why was she in her nightgown?

The only solution that made sense was that the woman had intended to drown herself.

I shan't touch anything, thought Paula as she looked closely at the bolt on the door, but I'm going to see what I can find.

The bolt was indeed very loose and had a tendency to slide towards the ENGAGED end when one moved the door sharply. So Cathy had been telling the truth about that, at least.

Mrs. Merton must have discovered this, too. Why, then, had she not pushed the chair against the door? Was this one of those suicide attempts that were intended to be discovered in time? Not very likely, since the only other person who used the bathroom was Cathy, and for all Mrs. Merton knew, she was going to be out all evening or might even have gone away. Presumably a cleaning woman would visit the bathroom in the morning, but by then the suicide attempt would have been successful.

No. If this was suicide, then it was for real.

An accident? This could not be ruled out. Perhaps she had had a stroke or a heart attack. But why did she get into the bath in her nightgown?

The inevitable conclusion was that she had not got into the bath of her own free will, but that somebody had put her there. Paula felt sure that Cathy had followed the same line of reasoning but did not want to admit it.

All the time these thoughts were going through her mind, Paula was looking round the bathroom.

In addition to the bath and the toilet there was a wash-basin fitted to the wall, with a wooden shelf above it. On this stood a bottle of scouring powder, a ragged piece of cloth, an old nail brush, and a glass tumbler with a little water at the bottom. Near the head of the bath was the solid old wooden chair. A white bath-towel, quite dry, hung over its back, and on the seat, trailing to the floor, was a pink quilted housecoat.

Still averting her eyes from the dead woman, Paula leant over to feel in the pockets of the housecoat. They were empty, but on the floor under the chair something light showed up against the dark green linoleum.

Paula crouched down to get a closer look. It was a little plastic cylinder, with what looked like a chemist's label stuck to it. If it had been made of glass, she thought, she would have been able to see how many capsules or tablets, if any, there were left inside it.

The temptation to pick up the container, unscrew the top, and examine the chemist's label was overwhelming. If I knew that she had swallowed a whole lot of Valium, said Paula to herself, maybe on top of whisky or gin, then the whole thing would make more sense. Getting into the bath would be to make completely sure. Only the previous day she had read in the evening paper of a man who had swallowed tranquillisers, consumed a quantity of alcohol, and then led a pipe from the exhaust into his car while it stood in the garage.

Such determined suicides spoke for themselves. If this was one of them, the problem would be to try to find out why she had done it. But surely it could be nothing at all to do with Cathy?

Unless Cathy had found Mrs. Merton drowned many hours earlier and had been too frightened to tell anybody.

For a moment or two Paula played with this idea. Given Cathy's reactions to the old woman, it seemed not entirely impossible. There was no reason at all to suspect Cathy of playing any part in the woman's death, but she could perhaps have found the body, much earlier in the day, before she came to the afternoon seminar, and not been able to face the ordeal on her own.

But that would mean that Cathy had not only neglected to carry out a possible life-saving, but had also sat through the entire seminar, making useful contributions to the discussion and showing no effects at all of the gruesome discovery she had just made.

Paula found it very difficult to believe this. She also found it impossible to believe that Cathy had taken such a roundabout way of leading her to the corpse, chatting over a leisurely tea, arriving only slowly, and with some embarrassment, at the problem over which she wished to consult Paula.

Nevertheless, she was taking a long time to fetch someone in authority. It was so quiet up here. Just the distant sound of somebody's radio or television from the floor below. All sorts of things could happen up here in this little eyrie and nobody else in the house would know. Not for a long time, at any rate.

The door of Cathy's room was open, as they had left it. The door of Mrs. Merton's room was shut. On a sudden impulse, Paula moved forward, stretched out her hand for the door-handle, hesitated, and, feeling rather foolish, caught hold of the end of her scarf and gripped the handle through it.

She had turned the handle and discovered that the door was un-locked when she heard the voices and footsteps on the floor below.

Just in time. Another minute up here by herself and she would have been caught snooping round Mrs. Merton's room, which would have taken a lot of explaining away.

CHAPTER 2

Joe Gainsborough's first reaction to the discovery of Mrs. Merton's body appeared to be anger rather than shock or distress.

"Why did the old cow have to go and drown herself here?" he muttered as he came into the bathroom. And then, "Yuk. No more lovely in death than in life. Sorry you got dragged into this, Paula. We don't usually greet our distinguished visitors to Bloomsbury Lodge with disgusting-looking corpses."

"I'm not a distinguished visitor," snapped Paula. "And surely death deserves some respect, even if it isn't pretty."

"Oh. Sorry." He looked at her with dislike. "Okay. Maybe she was somebody's mother, but it's a bloody nuisance all the same. We can do without this sort of thing at Bloomsbury Lodge."

"Anybody can do without it."

"We don't want the police poking around up here," went on Joe, ignoring her.

"Have the police been told?"

"Yes. An Inspector Beal will be here soon."

As he spoke he was looking round the bathroom, touching the rickety shelf, the wash-basins, the bath taps. For a moment Paula wondered whether he was trying to do some detective work himself, and then she believed she had guessed why he was so worried and so angry. It wasn't just because of Mrs. Merton; it was because of the general condition of the building, for which he and his wife were responsible. The lack of fire escapes, for example, which Paula herself had noticed; the faulty electric fittings, the shaky handrail on the stairs.

The place was full of death-traps, and even a cursory inspection would produce a long list of essential renovations. But Mrs. Merton had not fallen off the roof or been electrocuted or fallen downstairs, thought Paula, and if somebody had wanted to be rid of her they could have contrived a much more convincing accident than having her found dead in the bath.

This thought brought a little reassurance; it must surely be some sort of accident. Accident or suicide.

"Didn't Cathy come up with you?" she asked him.

"Yes." He grunted. He was examining the floor at the far end of the bath and didn't turn round. "I think she went to her room."

Paula left him to it and came out to look in Cathy's room. She was not there. After a moment's thought she came out onto the landing again and, forgetting all about fingerprints, pushed open the door of Mrs. Merton's room and walked straight in.

The room was similar to Cathy's, a large attic with a dormer window, bookshelves, a writing-table, a divan bed and chair, and a clothes closet. This closet was open and some of its contents laid out on the bed as if the occupant had started to pack. A big suitcase lay open on the floor, and beside it, kneeling on the threadbare carpet, was Cathy.

She glanced up when Paula came in, apparently not at all embarrassed at being discovered in such a position.

"We'll be in trouble if anybody finds us here," commented Paula.

Cathy merely smiled and put a finger to her lips. "Where's Joe Gainsborough?" she asked.

Paula shut the door before she replied. "He's creeping round the bathroom. Trying to conceal the neglect of ages. He's much more worried about the police getting onto the absence of safety precautions than he is about poor Mrs. Merton."

"I'm not surprised. Well, I guess that's not our worry. You won't tell anybody I've been in here, will you, Paula?"

"In this respect I'm your partner in crime. I only hope we can get out without being seen."

Cathy did not respond. She was looking thoughtful again. "It's quite gone," she said. "My spider horror of her, I mean. I just feel awfully sad. I wish I'd been kinder to her. I wish—oh, how I do wish —that I'd talked to her properly. Got to know her a little."

Paula looked sharply at the girl. She sounded perfectly sincere. A death always induces a certain sense of guilt, whether justified or not, among those remaining, and Cathy might well feel mildly sorry that she had not been friendlier to the old woman, but surely this grief and regret was excessive in the circumstances.

Cathy seemed to realise that she must divert Paula's thoughts.

"Look at those clothes," she said, getting to her feet.

Paula looked. The garments that lay on the bed were all black, of good quality but well worn. On a shelf in the closet was a little pile of underwear, and on the shelf above there was a hairbrush, silver-backed, and a comb and a hand mirror similarly decorated.

"She'd got some lovely things," said Cathy.

"Yes indeed."

Paula was puzzled. The clothes gave the impression of a lady's-maid in some stately home of many years ago, but the silver brushes seemed to speak more of the lady herself.

"It smells so musty," said Cathy.

"Mothballs. We'd better get out of here now, Cathy, while we've got the chance."

"I'll go first. Watch where I step. I know which of the floorboards don't creak."

The bathroom door was shut. They achieved Cathy's room without attracting Joe's attention.

"It's like a silly farce," said Paula, collapsing onto the bed.

"We made it," said Cathy, patting her on the back. Then suddenly she sobered up. "I've never seen anybody dead before. Have you?"

"Yes," replied Paula, "but only naturally and peacefully. Not sudden and unnatural."

"She looks so different. It's like a heap of trash lying on the floor there. It's not frightening at all. It's so terribly sad. Oh, if only I'd known!" Cathy sounded once more near to tears. "If only I'd really talked to her."

"Cathy," said Paula with all her suspicions reawakened, "why are you talking like this? What did you know about Mrs. Merton? I simply do not believe that you knew nothing about her."

"I'd never met her."

"Maybe, but that doesn't mean that she meant nothing to you."

There was no response.

"Listen," said Paula, "you asked me to help you, and I'm on your side. I've no idea what all this is about, yet you've obviously got a problem and I'll help you if I can. But you must be honest with me. Surely you can see that. How on earth can I help if you don't tell me the truth?"

"I haven't told you any lies," muttered Cathy. "Are you going to tell the police that you think I have?"

Paula hesitated, torn between sympathy and irritation. Cathy's sudden flood of tears swung her over to the former.

"It's shock," she said, feeling in her purse for a handkerchief. "I'm not feeling too good myself. Here you are, Cathy."

But the girl had got up from the bed and opened the top drawer of the battered old chest.

"I've got some here," she began, and then, with a complete change of voice, she cried, "Where's my watch? And my ring?"

In her agitation she pulled the drawer out too far and its contents spilled onto the floor. Paula helped her to pick up the mixture of pots and brushes, letters, scarves, gloves, and what looked like lecture notes.

"I'm sorry," said Cathy. "I can't seem to manage to keep things tidy."

"Neither can I," said Paula.

"Can't you? You look such a neat and efficient person."

"Purely superficial." Paula laughed. "Well, what are we going to do about your missing jewellery?"

"I could be mistaken," said Cathy doubtfully. "Maybe I didn't leave them in this drawer."

"Were they in a box?"

"The watch was. I can't remember about the ring."

It seemed to Paula, who had never possessed much in the way of valuables, that Cathy was taking the loss very lightly.

"It's my fault," the girl went on, "for being so careless. I ought to have taken them to the bank. I don't think I'll tell the police. I don't want to make a fuss. It's going to be quite bad enough, being asked about Mrs. Merton." Again she sounded near to tears.

"I think they are coming now," said Paula, going to the door and opening it a little way.

Cathy grabbed at her arm. "Don't leave me."

Paula shut the door again, turned to face Cathy, and tried to speak sternly, which was not easy, partly because she was several inches shorter than Cathy and partly because she herself was feeling very much in two minds. Half of her was longing to make her statement and get away from Bloomsbury Lodge as soon as possible, and this half felt angry with Cathy for dragging her into the affair. But the other half of her, the half that loved a mystery, knew that it would never rest until it had discovered the connection between the lovely and intelligent young American student and the shabby-genteel old Englishwoman.

Why had Cathy so feared her in life, so deeply and painfully regretted her death?

It was a question for the police, and Paula told the girl so. "But I am not going to mention it," she went on. "As far as I am concerned, you knew nothing about Mrs. Merton except that she was rather a nuisance as a neighbour. You weren't happy with your accommodation here, and you asked me, as your tutor, to help you find something more suitable. Will you stay with that story?"

"Yes," said Cathy in a low voice. "Thank you, Paula."

"And when they've finished with us, will you please tell me what you know about Mrs. Merton?"

"Yes. You know," went on Cathy in a rush, "I'm not usually secretive like this. But it's so terribly important to me. I've been longing to tell you, ever since you said you'd come to tea, but I didn't know how you'd react. I don't really understand English people, although I'm trying very hard."

"That's settled, then," said Paula. "It sounds as if they've finished with Joe for the time being and are coming our way."

She opened the door again. A tall, thin man with greying hair and faded blue eyes came out of the bathroom and introduced himself as Inspector Beal. Joe Gainsborough, looking very worried indeed, followed him. From inside the bathroom came the sound of movement and talking.

"Are you the ladies who found her?" asked the inspector in a tired voice.

Paula introduced herself and quickly explained.

Inspector Beal turned to Joe. "Have you somewhere quiet where we can talk?"

"There's my office in the basement. I'm sorry the lift's out of order."

The inspector, who was no longer young, did not look very pleased at the prospect of more footwork on the stairs.

"My room is right here." Cathy spoke for the first time. "There's only one chair, but it's quite tidy, so if you don't mind . . ."

Inspector Beal looked at her gratefully, and Paula began to hope that they might make their statements without arousing any suspicion that they were holding anything back. Indeed, the inspector's mind seemed to be running as much on the defects of Bloomsbury Lodge as on the sudden death of one of its residents, because he walked straight to the dormer window, opened it, leaned out, drew back, and said, "I thought as much" in a disgusted tone of voice before sitting down on the one chair.

It was made of wickerwork and it creaked ominously. Paula and Cathy exchanged glances and bit their lips to stifle the threat of nervous laughter. Fortunately the chair remained intact.

"I won't keep you long," said the inspector, seemingly unaware of his danger. "Can either of you tell me anything at all about Mrs. Merton?"

"I'm afraid not," replied Paula. "I never knew of her existence till I came here with Miss Bradshaw this afternoon to discuss her studies and to make sure that she had adequate accommodation, which is sometimes rather a problem for the overseas students."

"And Miss Bradshaw?"

Cathy looked all innocence. "I've spoken to her several times when we met on the stairs. She told me she was doing some research in the British Museum."

"Did she tell you anything about her life? Her circumstances?"

"Nothing at all. We never had any real talk."

"Did you form any impression of her?"

"Impression?" Cathy looked puzzled.

Inspector Beal tried again. "Did she strike you as a cheerful and contented sort of person?"

Potential suicide, thought Paula.

Cathy appeared to give this question her very serious consideration. "I just can't say," she said at last. "She was old and she was a bit lame, and I guess she was lonely, because she seemed to want to become acquainted with me, but that doesn't add up to her being unhappy. Maybe she was very unhappy, but I didn't see it. I just saw an old woman who was staying in Bloomsbury Lodge to be near the British Museum. She'd only been here a day or two. If she'd been here for longer I might have been able to tell you more."

Paula could detect signs of regret in these last words, regrets which the situation did not justify. Careful now, Cathy, she mentally urged the girl. Don't show any of those guilty and rueful feelings that you showed to me, or he'll never believe that you know nothing about Mrs. Merton.

"I'm sorry I can't help," muttered Cathy. "It's been a shock."

The danger moment was past; the rest of the interview went very smoothly. When Cathy described how she had managed to open the bathroom door the inspector's face took on an even more sour expression.

"I hope you don't think all English hostels and hotels are like this place," he said.

"Oh, I don't mind." Cathy said her little piece about liking old things and all things English, and the women's statements were completed in an atmosphere of goodwill.

Inspector Beal stood up. The wicker chair squealed its relief. "The inquest will probably be next week. I'll be in touch. Thank you for your co-operation."

He made a note of Paula's address, and paused at the door. "It's none of my business, Miss Bradshaw, but I don't think your parents would be very satisfied with your accommodation here. Can't you find somewhere else?"

"That's just what I've been telling her," interposed Paula before Cathy could reply. "We're going on to investigate a possibility now, if you don't need us any more."

After he had gone, Cathy sank with a sigh of relief into the worn-out chair, and continued to sink with it until the seat was on the floor.

"Help!" she cried, holding out her arms.

Paula pulled her up, and then they collapsed onto the bed in helpless laughter.

A knock at the door forced them to control themselves.

"Come in," called Cathy.

Carlos came in and looked at them in astonishment.

"We're recovering from the police enquiries," said Cathy, still laughing, "and from the chair."

She pointed to it. The dark boy did not smile.

"I have to speak to you," he said, looking keenly at Cathy.

Paula got up. "I'll wait downstairs. Then we'll go over to my office. We'll be able to talk there."

"Don't go. I'm coming, too," said Cathy. And then, turning to Carlos, "Can't it wait? Paula and I do have to discuss something urgently."

"It can wait," said the boy sullenly. "That's me. Always waiting."

"I'll be downstairs," repeated Paula firmly to Cathy. "Don't be too long." And as she moved past Carlos she added apologetically, "It really is important. Otherwise I wouldn't have asked Cathy to come."

She left the room without waiting for him to reply. From the bathroom came the sound of voices. Apparently the police had not yet finished in there. It seemed to Paula, as she came towards the attic stairs, that she had been up there at the top of the building for a very long time, and she was longing to be out of the place.

But this turned out to be not so easy. First she encountered two uniformed men, who looked like an ambulance crew. Then it seemed as if all the residents of the house, a fine mix of races and ages and accents, had congregated on the landings and in doorways to exchange misinformation about what was going on upstairs, and anybody coming down from the upper regions was eagerly seized upon.

"I can't tell you anything," said Paula again and again. "You'll have to ask Mr. Gainsborough."

The front door had been left open. Paula raced down the last flight of stairs and ran towards it, eager to escape. But there on the step was Marjorie Gainsborough, grey-haired, weary, and shocked and bewildered at the sight of the police vehicles outside the building.

"Paula Glenning!" she cried. "What are you doing here? What on earth's the matter?"

Paula summoned up all her reserves of patience. Mrs. Gainsborough was a talker, and in the circumstances she had every right to talk.

"I'm awfully sorry, Marjorie," she said, "but I've got an appointment and I'm terribly late already. There's been an accident to the old woman on the top floor. Joe's up there now with the police and the doctor. He'll be down in a minute and will tell you all about it. I shouldn't go up if I were you. There's an awful crowd up there."

She tried again to make her escape, but Marjorie barred the way.

"Accident? What sort of accident? Has Joe—" She broke off and clapped a hand to her mouth. Above it, her eyes looked very alarmed.

"Joe is all right," said Paula gently. "It was I who found her. She seems to have drowned in her bath. I don't know how or why."

Mrs. Gainsborough seemed to relax a little. "Perhaps she slipped. She was slightly disabled."

"I expect that was it," said Paula.

The way was now open for her to leave, but whereas a moment ago she had been desperate to get out of the building, now she felt inclined to linger. What had Marjorie been about to say in that first moment of shock when she began "Has Joe—" and then hurriedly controlled herself? What did she imagine Joe might have done? Was it simply one of the many sins of omission—the dripping taps, the faulty electrical fittings unattended to—or was it something more positive and more sinister?

"Did you know anything about Mrs. Merton?" she asked.

"No, I didn't. What was there to know?" countered Mrs. Gainsborough, quite sharply for so indeterminate a person.

It was obvious that there were to be no more revelations now. Further questions would only arouse suspicion, particularly as Paula had declared that she had not a moment to spare.

"I must fly," she said, feeling both foolish and insincere. "I'm sure it will all be cleared up soon. Goodbye."

Outside in the roadway a small crowd had gathered to stare at the police cars and ambulance and wait for something to happen. Paula pushed her way through to the quiet and darkness of the gardens and sat down on a bench from which she could see the entrance to Bloomsbury Lodge. She was sure, or almost sure, that Cathy would keep her appointment, but nevertheless she felt that the sooner they were together again, the better.

Besides, there might be something to be learned from watching the house.

Nothing happened for at least ten minutes, apart from a taxi driving up and discharging a middle-aged couple with an incredible number of suitcases. Incoming residents, thought Paula, and tried to imagine their feelings on arriving at such a moment. This surely ought to bring Cathy out, because Carlos would have to come down to attend to the new arrivals.

Her reasoning was accurate. A few minutes later Cathy appeared on the doorstep, looked around her with a somewhat bewildered air, and then made her way across the road.

Paula got up to meet her at the entrance to the gardens. "I thought I'd wait for you here. It's best not to walk across alone at night."

Cathy looked incredulous. "You don't get rapes here?"

"You do indeed. And other nasties, too. Come out of your dream, Cathy. London is no earthly paradise. It's a violent, dangerous capital city. No better than anywhere else."

"I don't believe it. Not here in Bloomsbury."

Paula decided that this was not the best moment to pursue the subject, although it struck her yet again how vulnerable Cathy was in her romantic illusions about England.

"Tell me about Carlos," Paula said as they walked together into the deeper darkness under the trees.

"He's okay. He's half American and half Mexican. He's come to London to study economics. Mr. Gainsborough is teaching him in his Open University seminar, and they let him live here without paying in exchange for duties at the enquiry desk."

"He has to work hard," commented Paula.

"Sure he works hard, and he's bright, too, but he's very jealous. Two-ways jealous. He doesn't like seeing me with anybody else, either male or female, and he doesn't like me being a post-graduate student because it means I'm ahead of him in the academic marathon."

"He sounds rather like Joe Gainsborough," said Paula, "who doesn't like Marjorie being better qualified than he is. It's a rare man who genuinely does not resent an academic female."

"Have you found that yourself?" asked Cathy.

Paula made the little speech that she usually made in reply to this type of question. "Though that was not the main reason for my marriage failure," she said, "I think it's one of the reasons I don't want to commit myself again. It's very selfish of me, but I feel there's a sort of restraint, as if one can never really let oneself go, never find out what one is capable of, when one makes a close permanent relationship."

Although I never feel like that with James, she added silently to herself. How very strange. Not until this moment did she fully realise how undemanding he really was. She was overcome by a wave of affection for him, and almost hoped that they would find him still in their shared office.

But the building was in darkness, and Paula had to unlock the front door and that of her office. It smelt of cigarette smoke, Paula's desk chair had been turned round to form part of a circle, a wastepaper basket had been knocked over, its contents spilling to the floor, and there was a general air of disorder in the room.

Paula smiled to herself. James, who was inclined to be fastidious, occasionally complained about her smoking and her untidiness and threatened to leave the room as he sometimes found it. It looked as if he had chosen this afternoon to carry out the threat.

"Draw the curtains, Cathy," she said, "and I'll go and see if Dr. Goff has left us any sherry. If not, it will have to be coffee. We need something to revive us. Shan't be long."

A few minutes later she returned from the pantry with two steaming mugs. "Sorry I've nothing to offer you to eat," she said.

"Thanks. I don't feel hungry."

"Neither do I. Finding dead bodies seems to take away your appetite."

Cathy took a sip and then placed her mug on James's desk and propped herself on the clear space beside it.

"Look," she said, "what Carlos brought me."

She held out a hand towards Paula. In the palm lay a tiny wrist-watch, diamond-studded, and a ring with a single ruby.

"Carlos?" repeated Paula. "Did he steal them?"

"I shouldn't think so. He wouldn't do that to me. He knows I'd help him if he was short of cash."

This was not said in any boastful manner, but with the casualness of somebody to whom money had never been a problem. Up till now Paula had assumed that, like so many students from overseas, Cathy was better off than her English counterparts, but by no means wealthy. The choice of accommodation confirmed this judgment, and in general Cathy appeared to live very modestly. But now Paula began to wonder.

"Where did Carlos find them?" she asked.

"In the drawer of the reception desk. He'd seen me wearing the watch, so he knew they were mine." Cathy returned the items to the pocket of her jacket. "He doesn't know who put them there, but it could have been almost anybody in the building. That's why it was chosen."

"A good place to get rid of stolen property in a hurry?"

"That's right."

Paula suggested that Carlos might have taken the jewellery in order to ingratiate himself with Cathy by returning it to her, but Cathy rejected this theory.

"He doesn't need to act like that. He's helped me a lot and he knows I'm grateful to him."

She took a drink of coffee, got off James's desk, and came to sit in one of the armchairs near to Paula.

"Let's forget about Carlos for the present. I just can't wait any longer to tell you my story. How do you want it? Straight from the beginning, in chronological order, like a nineteenth-century novel, with all the dull bits left in? Or all jazzed up to hold the attention, so that you only get the meat of it in a series of flashbacks?"

"Like a Victorian novel, please," said Paula.

Cathy smiled briefly. "That suits me fine." But then she seemed to change her mind and withdraw into herself, saying nothing, but cradling her mug in her hands and staring at the dark green carpet.

CHAPTER 3

On the other side of the square, Bloomsbury Lodge residents were eating their dinner and the house was gradually returning to normal.

In Paula's office, Cathy looked up at last and said, "No, not a Victorian novel. I'm going to start at the end."

She placed the mug on the floor, put a hand in her jacket pocket, pulled out a small square of red leather, and handed it to Paula, who opened it out and saw that it held an old photograph in fading mono-chrome. The picture was of two young men of the pre-Beatles era, with cropped hair and wearing baggy trousers and polo-necked sweaters.

Paula extracted the photograph from the frame and turned it over. On the back was written in a large, neat sloping hand, "Frank and Bill before they went to America."

"Well?" Paula replaced the snapshot in the frame and made a movement to hand it back to Cathy.

"No, keep it while I tell you," said the girl. "It'll take quite a long time. That's why I'm giving you the punch line first. Wait for it. I believe Mrs. Merton was my grandmother."

Paula looked suitably surprised, but in fact she had been half ex-pecting some sort of revelation of this nature.

"Now we are going back," went on Cathy, "twenty-three years to San Francisco, where I was born. But when I was still very young I was brought to Boston, where my mother's folks live. Do you know Boston?"

"I've stayed there with a former colleague of mine, now at Har-vard."

"Then you'll know something of the life-style. My stepfather is a lawyer. He's twenty years older than my mother and they have two children. Both boys. They have a lovely home and a full social life and they reared me to be an all-American girl and a credit to them."

She looked up at Paula and smiled faintly. "I can see you wondering why I say 'they' and not 'we.' Of course it was my home, too, my only home, but I was never part of it. I was the outsider. I was never badly treated, but I always knew they would rather I had not been there. I reminded them of my father, you see, and they would have liked to forget him."

Cathy paused for a moment, sipped at her coffee, and stared at Paula without seeing her.

"Before my mother married," she went on, "we lived in a very different sort of environment, students sharing. A sort of commune, you might call it."

Paula nodded, and Cathy continued, "I don't remember much about it, but I do just remember my father."

She smiled again, not wryly this time, but with a warmth and glow that transformed her face. Even under strain and tension she was a very pretty girl, but in joyful emotion she was stunning.

"We had a black-and-white cat called Pompey," she said. "I remember him most clearly of all, and it is through Pompey that I just remember my father. I was always wanting to stroke Pompey and he was always jumping up on top of things out of my reach. He was on top of a bookcase. I can see him sitting there—black fur and white face and whiskers—and I can see hands reaching out for him and picking him up and stroking him and holding him on the floor for me to stroke. Just hands. Kind hands. Gentle and strong and safe hands. That's all I remember of my father."

Cathy was now leaning forward in her chair, chin propped on her palms, staring into memory.

Paula, waiting for her to speak again, opened up the photograph frame once more and stared at the snapshot with renewed interest. Presumably one of these very out-of-date-looking boys was Cathy's father. Which one? Did Cathy herself know the answer to that question?

"He left us," said Cathy presently. "I don't know why, but we never saw him again. He wrote once, not to my mother, but to his friend Bill Prescott. He wrote from an address in London."

"Bloomsbury Lodge," said Paula.

"Bloomsbury Lodge," repeated Cathy. "It wasn't my mother who told me this. It was Bill Prescott. Uncle Bill. He didn't keep the letter, but he told me about it. It said, 'Lousy flight. London looking very drab and Dickens-like. I'll stay a day or two and then go down to the old village. Enclosed card is for Cathy.'

"The card he enclosed for me," went on Cathy, "which I did see and I remember quite clearly, was a sketch of Buckingham Palace and Westminster Abbey and the Tower of London all jumbled up together, with a little man in the centre hung all over with cameras, gawking at everything. My father studied history, but he was very clever at drawing. Uncle Bill told me this."

"Have you got the card?" asked Paula.

"No," said Cathy sadly. "My mother took it away from me and I never saw it again. She wouldn't listen to me if I ever asked about him, and after she got married—I guess I was five or six years old then—I never tried to speak to her about him again. At least not in my stepfather's house. I was told not to speak to Bill Prescott about him either. My mother didn't want to remember her wild past."

The sixties, thought Paula. The hippies, the flower children, student revolt. A picture of Cathy's origins was beginning to take shape in her mind. The two English boys leaving their own country in search of love and joy and wisdom across the Atlantic, joining up with their counterparts on the other side. Cathy herself, and maybe others as well, was an inevitable result.

Then later the father, for a reason yet to be discovered, returned to his own country, wrote once from London, and was never heard of again. Not to Cathy's knowledge, at any rate. The mother, once a rebel against her own orthodox upbringing, reverted to type and made a very suitable marriage. If the daughter had inherited the mother's looks, then the mother herself must have been a very pretty girl. She had quickly adapted again to her natural element, but the child could not adjust so easily. She clung to her own origins and to her one dim memory of her own father.

"But at least your mother did give you this photograph," said Paula. "I can well understand that it is very precious to you."

"Oh no." Cathy came out of her reverie. "My mother never gave me this. She tried to destroy every memory of my father."

"Then where did you get it from?"

Cathy did not reply. The glow had gone from her face and she was looking rather nervous.

"From your father's friend?"

Cathy shook her head. "Don't be angry, Paula. I know I ought not to have done it, but when I found it in her room . . . It meant so much to me."

"Cathy! You took this photo from Mrs. Merton's room?"

"Yes. Just before you came in. It was with her hairbrushes. I guess those were her precious things on that shelf. I didn't leave any finger-prints, honest, Paula, and we got out of there without anybody see-ing us."

"I most certainly hope we did." Paula was startled, not so much by Cathy's revelations in themselves but by the fact that the girl was prepared to take very positive action, even illegal action, in following up her romantic dream. "You do realise that for all we know this could turn out to be a murder investigation?"

Cathy nodded, very wide-eyed.

"And that tampering with evidence can be a serious offence?"

"Yes, I know. But to find this—oh, Paula! Don't you know—can't you guess—what it feels like not to know who you really are?"

The search for identity, thought Paula. Yes, that, too, was part of the ethos of that generation. Catherine Bradshaw, a child of the sixties, an illegitimate child, a mixed-up child, rejecting the security of her mother's world and searching for what she felt to be her origins across the Atlantic.

Yes, of course she could understand the sort of driving force that would lead such a child to follow her dream, the same sort of force that drove many an adopted child to search for the natural mother. But how terribly vulnerable it made the searcher. How could even the most fortunate of realities possibly measure up to the dream?

Indeed, it was only too likely that this gifted girl, with her bril-liant, butterfly-like beauty, her secure social position, her excellent prospects, was going to end up by uncovering some wretched, sordid little story.

Paula longed to stop her before it was too late. But there was no turning back now. Cathy was hot on the trail of her own origins, and neither fear nor conscience nor anything else was going to stand in her way. All Paula could do was to go along with her and try, maybe, now and then to modify her expectations.

But first of all she must hear the full story.

"Which one of these," she asked, pointing to the snapshot, "is your father's friend?"

"The one on the left. Bill Prescott, whom I've always called Uncle Bill. He hasn't changed all that much over the years."

Paula studied the photograph more closely. It looked as if it had been taken on a cloudy day in somebody's backyard. Behind the boys was the wall of a house, revealing a drain-pipe and a piece of sloping roof. Cathy's Uncle Bill was not quite as tall as the man on the right, but otherwise the two were of much the same build. Both looked lively and intelligent, with good features, but here again the one on the right hand had the advantage: a dark, striking-looking young man; a character to be reckoned with. But was there any resemblance to Cathy?

"Uncle Bill," said Cathy, "must have known how much I needed him after my dad went away. He got friendly with my stepfather's housekeeper, and she fixed it for us to meet. The risks they took!" She laughed. "It was easier when I was older. He could come and fetch me from school. And in any case he'd become respectable himself by then. He married a Boston girl and became an American citizen and got a teaching job at the University of Virginia and moved to Charlottesville. That's why I went there myself. To be near Uncle Bill. Mother didn't like it, but my stepfather was glad to be rid of me. I never quarrel with my stepfather. We just don't relate. We run along parallel lines. He knew I was never going to fit in with his life-style and he accepted it."

"Did you fit in in Virginia?" asked Paula curiously.

"Well no, not really, because I don't really feel I belong anywhere. But I can adapt to most things and I enjoyed my studies. And of course I spent a lot of time at Uncle Bill's house."

"What did his wife have to say about that?" wondered Paula aloud.

Cathy assured her that there was no jealousy. "I knew plenty of men my own age. Uncle Bill was like a father to me. He still kept his British accent, after all those years, and I tried to imitate it. Had you noticed?" asked Cathy eagerly.

"Yes, I noticed. You're doing very well," said Paula. "Was Bradshaw your mother's name?"

"That's right. The man she married wanted me to have his name, but my mother's parents wanted me to keep theirs. They'd built up a sort of myth about my father, you see, pretending that he hadn't left my mother but that she had left him. Or rather, she had been forced to choose between her homeland and her lover, and she had chosen her homeland. And so off he went alone, since she would not come with him, crazy with grief and leaving me behind as a sort of tragic heroine of romance."

"A Wilkie Collins novel," put in Paula.

"I just call it the Bradshaw Version. They're both dead now, and they left me—well, just let's say they left me a lot of money. So I'm independent and don't have to account for my actions to anybody."

"And you chose Bloomsbury Lodge rather than rent an apartment or stay in a hotel."

"It seemed the obvious place to begin. And I wanted to live as my father would have lived. He came from a little village near Oxford— Wilsham—and his folks were very poor. Uncle Bill came from Yorkshire. I don't think his folks were very prosperous either, but they're mostly dead now, I think."

"If you do find your father," began Paula carefully, wondering how best to voice a suspicion that was growing in her mind, "and if he is in any way in need—"

"Then I'm going to help him, of course," said Cathy, thus saving Paula the trouble of feeling for her words.

This fervent declaration of Cathy's put a new complexion on the whole business. Cathy's search, even if she had not been a wealthy girl, would have exposed her to all sorts of shocks and disappointments, but to come as an heiress with the deliberate intention of dispensing largesse to poor relations opened up alarming possibilities. How could she be so naive and so rash? To Paula it sounded like an open invitation to fraud and imposture.

"I know what you're thinking," said Cathy, watching her closely, "but honestly, Paula, I'm being careful. Maybe I am a bit casual about my trinkets, but I promise you I'm no fool when it comes to money."

Paula could only hope this was true. "What does Uncle Bill think of your pilgrimage?" she asked.

"He didn't like it." Cathy frowned. "He said he could understand why I wanted to come and he thought it a good idea to get it out of my system, but he didn't think I'd much chance of finding my father on my own, not after all this time. He says he never knew why my father decided to head out for England again without giving any warning, but I'm not so sure about that."

"You think he's not told you the truth?"

"About everything else I'm sure he's speaking the truth," replied Cathy, "but about my father's leaving us . . . No, I guess he's hiding something. Maybe to protect my mother. Maybe to protect himself."

"You mean," said Paula carefully, "that your mother had, shall we say, switched her affection to Bill Prescott and your father was rejected? That that was why he went away, and your grandparents were perhaps not so very wrong after all?"

"I don't know." Cathy took back the precious photograph and sat brooding over it. "I don't want to think it. I love Uncle Bill. More than anybody else in the world. He's been the most important person in my life. And I trust him. All the way. Except over this. And that's why I wanted to come here alone."

Alone. Paula repeated the word to herself. This was the most striking thing about Cathy Bradshaw. Not her beauty, nor her character, nor her wealth, but her quite alarming aloneness in her enterprise. How could her "Uncle Bill," if he cared for her as much as he seemed to, have allowed her to embark on such an undertaking without some sort of protection? If Cathy herself refused help, surely Bill Prescott could have arranged for somebody to keep an eye on her?

"Did he give you any sort of clues to follow up?" she asked, once again carefully feeling her way.

"Oh yes. The address in Wilsham where my father's folks used to live. I went there the day after I arrived in England. It was Church

Lane, but it had disappeared. There were a lot of new houses, and nobody I spoke to even remembered it."

"Was there a village post office? A pub? A vicarage?"

"I thought of all these," said Cathy. "There was a little row of shops, quite new, and they didn't know anything either and weren't very friendly. The woman in the pub couldn't help, but she was quite kind and she sent me on to the vicar. He had only been there for a few months, but he made a note of it and said he'd try to find out and would write to me. He thought I was one of those Americans trying to trace their ancestry," Cathy added with a smile, "and I didn't disillusion him."

"He'll look in the parish registers," said Paula. "It won't be much trouble for him and you ought to be hearing from him soon. I take it you know your father's name?"

"Frank Merton," murmured Cathy.

"I see. So the name did mean something to you from the first."

"Only that it was the same, and that Mrs. Merton came to Bloomsbury Lodge. It's not an uncommon name, but I must admit that I got a bit of a shock when Carlos told me, and I couldn't help wondering. And then I thought, the fact that my father came here twenty years ago, and that an old woman of the same name came here now—well, was that something so very remarkable? But of course my mind was so full of it, and when she seemed to be so interested in me—"

She broke off, and hesitated for a moment before going on.

"Paula, I'm sorry if I seemed to be not quite honest with you. It's partly that I didn't know you well and didn't know how you would react, and I couldn't bear to have my story laughed at. And partly because I felt so confused."

Paula murmured encouragement.

"One part of me was longing for her to be something to do with me, but the rest of me was scared. I'd been hoping and dreaming so much, but when it actually came to the point, it's like—it's like opening up a box when you don't know what's in it. Or opening a door. I guess I was scared to be on the track of the truth. And she was so—so . . . Oh, Paula, I did find her repulsive! But if she really was my grandmother! Oh, Paula!"

Cathy buried her face in her hands, then raised it for a moment to ask whether they could have some more coffee. By the time Paula had returned with the re-filled mugs, she had recovered herself.

"That's nearly it," she said. "I told Carlos I'd be back by nine, and it's twenty to now."

"Can it possibly be so early?" said Paula, looking at her watch. "I feel as if I've been immersed in the affair of Mrs. Merton for a lifetime."

"You'll soon be free of it. And I just don't know how to thank you. I'm quite okay now, and all I want to say is that I've been thinking it over ever since I found that photo and I can't help wondering whether Uncle Bill did know all along where my father was now and that he wrote to him and fixed it for him to find me here to give me a lovely surprise."

"Bill Prescott might do that sort of thing?"

"Yes," replied Cathy. "He's a great guy for springing lovely surprises. I'm not too keen on them myself."

"Nor I. I'd rather have things done in a straightforward way. But at least it does make sense. I've found it very difficult to believe that he would let you come alone like this without some arrangements for your protection."

"If it's true, then I don't like his arrangements," said Cathy. "It's treating me like a child."

"I quite agree. I wouldn't like it either. Presumably you were meant to amuse yourself doing detective work at Bloomsbury Lodge, and after a short interval Frank Merton was to turn up in person to claim his long-lost daughter."

"But he didn't come."

"No. His mother came instead. And before you could get to know each other, she was dead."

They were silent for a moment, both thinking hard.

"Is it just a coincidence?" said Cathy at last. "Or is it possible that just my being here trying to find my father resulted in Mrs. Merton dying?"

"If only we could find out," began Paula, knowing now that she herself would never rest until she had found the answer to Cathy's question. "But of course," she went on hastily, seeing that Cathy was looking very distressed, "we don't know how or why she died. There are so many possibilities. An accident is far the most likely, but she might perhaps have killed herself, or somebody else might have played a part in it. If we were in a murder story looking for opportunity, why, there it is, wide open. Dozens of people in Bloomsbury Lodge. All the time coming and going. And look how remote and secluded that attic floor is."

"Let's think of possibilities," said Cathy, trying to smile. "Joe Gainsborough. She'd been threatening to tell his wife about his lady friends."

"Or to tell the fire inspector about the state of the house."

"That's a better motive for *Mrs.* Gainsborough," said Cathy, "and she's just the sort of downtrodden character who could easily break out one day."

"You see? We've got two possibilities already. There must be loads more. What about Carlos?"

"Carlos!" Cathy got quickly to her feet. "I'll have to go. I can't keep him waiting again."

On the way downstairs Paula said, "Have you told Carlos all that you've told me?"

"Not about my father. Only that I want to find somebody who was at Bloomsbury Lodge twenty years ago. He's helped me a lot."

"In what way?"

"He's found out who was the warden at the time when my father came here. He told me when he came upstairs just now, and he's going to try to find out more. It's a Dr. Arnold Frend, a historian. The address is in Oxford." She named the street. "Does it mean anything to you, Paula? I don't want to bother you any more with my affairs, but I thought you might know something about him."

"I'm afraid I don't. It's before my time, and I don't know many historians. But I could do some research for you. And don't apologise for bringing me into your affairs. I do feel very concerned for you. I hope you won't think I'm being interfering when I beg you to be very careful. With everybody. With Carlos, too."

"He doesn't make too good an impression at first," said Cathy, "but he's okay. Honest, Paula."

"Not only with Carlos," said Paula as they came out of the front door, "but if somebody turns up who you think might be—"

"The man I'm looking for," Cathy concluded for her. "Don't worry, dear Paula. I'm very cautious. Look how cautious I was over Mrs. Merton. I guess I could spot an imposter even if I didn't have this photo. It's about the only thing that I really am quite sure of— that this is a picture of my dad."

"Keep it safe, then, for God's sake. And don't forget, if the police start asking any more questions, you just stick to the story you told this afternoon. Heaven knows how we are going to get through the inquest. We'll be lying our heads off in the witness-box, both of us."

"That's not till next week. Anything might have happened by then."

"It might indeed. Good night, Cathy. Take care."

Cathy ran down the steps, turned at the bottom, and blew Paula a kiss. Then she crossed the road and was almost instantly out of sight in the darkness of the gardens.

Paula looked anxiously after her. Did Cathy just refuse to believe that there had been attacks on young women in the square gardens at night? Or was she brave to the point of foolhardiness? Probably the latter, thought Paula. To set out on such a mission at all implied a very determined character. Besides, Cathy had talked openly about a spider phobia and several times said she was scared, and Paula was of the opinion that to admit to fear was itself a sign of courage.

For several minutes Paula stood on the doorstep, telling herself not to worry so much about Cathy. It was impossible, from where she stood, to see the entrance to Bloomsbury Lodge, and in any case Cathy had probably arranged to meet Carlos in the gardens.

There was nothing more that she could do. It was past nine o'clock, and James was supposed to be coming to a meal at her flat at nine. He had a key, and she hoped that he would think to make it ready, for suddenly she was exceedingly hungry, and so exhausted that she hardly knew how to collect her Mini from the college car park and achieve the twenty-minute drive home.

CHAPTER 4

James had bought a bottle of rosé and had taken the cold meats and salads out of the fridge and set the kitchen table. Paula gave him a brief hug, put a couple of radishes into her mouth, managed to say through them, "Tell you later," and disappeared into the bathroom.

When she got back to the kitchen he was sitting there placidly doing a crossword puzzle and crunching cheese biscuits.

"I'm hungry," he said in the mildest of protests.

"So am I."

How he has changed, she thought, over the last few years. It was difficult to remember that she had once thought him intolerably selfish. But so he had been, during the time following the breakdown of her own marriage, when she had more or less drifted into a relationship with James that could lead nowhere and only cause fresh pain.

Perhaps the change had begun during the time when James had wanted to marry the girl who looked after his famous novelist grandfather. He had started off for purely selfish reasons, but had later come truly to love her, and the affair had ended tragically.*

That, looking back from the present vantage point, had been the end of Paula's being in love with James and the start of her regarding him as a very good friend. Events in her life since then† had greatly strengthened her own career and increased her confidence; and during these years they had become, slowly and almost imperceptibly, more and more at ease with each other and had got into the habit of sharing their lives, staying sometimes in Paula's little flat, sometimes in James's more luxurious apartment.

It was a very comfortable, companionable, and undemanding sort of relationship, and as far as Paula was concerned it could stay like

* See *Last Judgment.*
† See *Cabin 3033* and *The Mystery Lady.*

that indefinitely. But in her wiser moments she realised that nothing could ever stop still, and that what suited both of them so well now might not suit one or the other of them at all in two years' time. In fact, James was already suggesting a more permanent commitment. Paula knew, although he never actually admitted it, that he dreaded growing old. He had been a clever and handsome spoilt child for the first fifteen years of his life and a clever and handsome young man for the next twenty-five. What was to come next? Surely only a decline.

Paula herself had no fear of aging nor, for most of the time, had she much dread of loneliness. But in the moods of depression that attacked her without warning from time to time, she would picture to herself a life without James in it, and the thought was unendurable. It was during such moods, when she felt such an overwhelming need for comfort, that she most dreaded taking a false step.

To be tempted into another big mistake was her secret dread, just as to be old and alone was James's, but these were matters that were never mentioned between them. Perhaps one day they would be able to talk freely of their deepest fears; but if that time ever came, it would mean that they had both changed very much indeed.

It seemed that James was capable of change; more so, thought Paula, than she was herself. Or perhaps she had changed more than she realised. Sometimes she thought she would like to ask him whether she had, but it never seemed to be quite the moment.

"I don't know what you would do without me," said James as they settled down to eat. "You need somebody to look after you. Why don't we get married and buy a nice new Victorian-style town house in Kensington and hire a housekeeper and give intellectual dinner parties and live graciously. You're a big girl now. It's time you stopped living in a draughty attic *à la bohème.*"

"I don't like gracious living," said Paula. "Besides, Rosie wouldn't want to move."

Rosie was James's black cat.

"All right, then. We'll get married and live in my flat."

"We'd be murdering each other within the week."

The conversation ran its usual course; it had taken place many times before. Paula wanted to make it end differently, but could not find the words. It was as if their relationship had got stuck in a groove. It was a relief to her when James concluded, as he always did, "All right, then. When we are both sixty we are going to give ourselves the unique retirement present of going through a ceremony at Hampstead Register Office. Meanwhile I cannot imagine how you are going to thank me for all I do for you."

"I'm going to tell you a story," said Paula.

"Not the one about the professor of Latin and the student from Tonga? I heard it in the common room this morning."

"No, no. A real story about a beautiful girl with a mysterious past, and a missing man who may be a villain, and a body in the bath."

"I heard rumours of the last-named," said James, pouring out more wine for them both. "I might have known you'd have got yourself involved in it. Bloomsbury Lodge, wasn't it? Whatever were you doing there, anyway?"

"Having tea with a student."

"Very rash." James shook his head. "These quaint, old-fashioned amusements always lead to trouble. You'd have done much better to take him to the pub."

"It wasn't a him, it was a her. Cathy Bradshaw. You met her at the dean's sherry party. You couldn't keep your eyes off her."

James began to look interested. "Gorgeous girl. But very aloof. Obviously not interested in middle-aged dons."

"Nor in young students either, according to one of her admirers in my seminar. There's only one man in the world for her, and he may not even exist."

"And who is that?" asked James obligingly.

"Her dead old dad. Now listen."

James was a good listener, and he seized at once on a point that had been worrying Paula more and more.

"This photograph is the only firm evidence that Mrs. Merton is in any way connected with Cathy's father?"

"Yes."

"And Cathy herself had no doubt at all that one of the men in the picture was her father's friend?"

"None. Neither have I. The photo meant a very great deal to her."

"It would, in the circumstances, but photos can be planted. Or—

more likely in this case—photos can be stolen and used to back up the claims of somebody posing as somebody else."

"Exactly," said Paula. "I'm so glad that's occurred to you, too. Cathy has money and is dying to find some poor English relations to give it to. She's never met any of them; she knows nothing about them except what her Uncle Bill has told her. An excellent opportunity for somebody to get hold of some cash."

"Well done, Paula," said James. "You're learning fast. You never used to believe that most people are motivated by greed."

"You taught me." She leaned across the little kitchen table and kissed him. "Not by being one of them, but by being a notable exception. And I believe Cathy is an exception to that rule as well. I can't bear to think of her coming to any harm, and I really do want to know what became of Frank Merton."

"Me, too. And I'd also like to know how the body got into the bath."

"If you really do want to help . . ." began Paula doubtfully.

"Of course I do. I wouldn't miss your sleuthing activities for the world. Maybe we'll be able to arrange another car chase," added James hopefully.

"Heaven forbid. But I did think we might go down to Oxford tomorrow afternoon and call on Dr. Arnold Frend."

"Excellent idea, and tomorrow morning—"

He was interrupted by the telephone ringing. Paula went into the living-room to answer it, and was followed by James carrying their coffee-cups.

"Oh, Marjorie," James heard her say, "I'm awfully sorry I didn't stop longer to talk to you this evening. No, of course it's not too late to call me—I never go to bed till midnight. . . . You saw the inspector? . . . Yes, I know Joe was very upset. . . . Yes, it was a nasty shock, but I don't feel any the worse for it. . . . You know how she died? An overdose? Well, I did wonder. . . . How did you find out?"

James came to sit on the settee beside Paula, put an arm round her shoulders and an ear close to the telephone. A very agitated woman's voice was to be heard on the line.

"I don't think Dr. Graham is really supposed to talk about it, but

I've known him for years. He's only recently taken up police work. He knew I was worried to death. It looks as if the wretched woman was taking tranquillisers and swallowed too many of them and got into the bath in a bemused state."

"Thank goodness for that," said Paula.

"Yes, isn't it awful?" said Marjorie Gainsborough. "But I feel exactly the same. I ought to feel sorry about it, but after all, I didn't even know her, and I'm just so relieved that there seems to be no question of—"

"Of anything but an accident?"

"Yes. We've got quite enough problems with all the repairs that we're going to have to do. And as for the fire inspector—and you know what the committee is like. They're living in 1945. They haven't a notion what things cost nowadays. Anyway, that's not what I phoned for. What I wanted to know was, Paula, is Cathy Bradshaw with you by any chance?"

James felt Paula stiffen. "Cathy Bradshaw? No, why should she be with me?"

"I thought you might have taken her home with you," said Marjorie, "since you'd been through that awful experience together, and I didn't think she'd want to sleep up there in the attic, not after what happened, and I was going to suggest that she could have the spare room in my flat for the night, and next week I could find her another room, because several people are leaving earlier than they intended, and I'm getting rather worried about her because it's not a pleasant thing to happen, is it, in the place where you are staying."

The anxious voice trickled on relentlessly. Paula, who had been making faces of despair at James as she tried to get a word in, managed to interrupt at last.

"Cathy is all right. She came over to my office for a while and then she was going on out to dinner or to a show."

"I wish she'd told me."

"But why should she tell you?" asked Paula, suddenly feeling very irritable with poor Marjorie. "I thought your residents were assumed to be going out unless they actually signed in for a meal."

"I thought she'd come down to see me," said Marjorie, ignoring Paula's remark. "Once the police had gone. After all, Joe and I are responsible for the welfare of the residents, and when something like this happens . . ."

Paula thought that she was beginning to understand. Mrs. Gainsborough was one of those people who conceal their real thoughts and feelings under a mass of irrelevancies. What she really wanted now was to have Cathy's version of the finding of Mrs. Merton's body. Why? Surely Marjorie, of all people, could not be in any way involved? Unless she was not so innocent as she seemed. And not so simple. It had taken a tortuous sort of cleverness, for example, to drag that information about the overdose out of the doctor.

"Marjorie," said Paula aloud, not listening to what the other was saying, "can I come and see you tomorrow morning?"

"Yes, of course. Join me for coffee. But if this man telephones for Cathy again—"

"Phoning for Cathy? You never told me."

"I've just been trying to tell you," said Marjorie, with the strained patience of one who doesn't expect to be listened to. "He's called twice this evening. An uncle of hers, I believe he said."

"From Charlottesville, Virginia? Did he speak with an English accent?"

"Well, sort of. How did you know?"

"Did he leave any message?"

"Only for her to call him back as soon as she came in. But she hasn't come in, and it's getting late, and I don't know what to say to him if he phones again."

"If he rings again," Paula began, and then she added, in an agitated whisper, "Hi—stop that! Let go!"

James in his eagerness to hear, had been pulling the telephone away from her.

"What did you say?" came a puzzled voice from the other end of the line.

"Sorry," said Paula. "It's the cat. She loves cutting off people's telephone calls in the middle by dancing on the phone."

"I didn't know you had a cat," said Marjorie.

James began to laugh. Paula grabbed the phone, got up, and retreated behind the settee.

"Listen, Marjorie," she said, keeping a wary eye on James. "I know all about Cathy's uncle who is trying to get in touch with her, and if he calls again, the best thing is for you to give him my number and tell him you think Cathy is with me. I have a feeling she may be turning up at my flat tonight."

"Lies, downright lies," muttered James.

Marjorie Gainsborough poured out her gratitude and relief to Paula. She had more than enough to cope with at the moment without the worry of Cathy on top of it.

"I'm sure she's all right," said Paula when she could make herself heard. "Just tell her uncle to phone me if he rings again."

A fresh account of the troubles at Bloomsbury Lodge threatened. James stretched out a hand and cut it off.

"You shouldn't have done that," said Paula. "Poor Marjorie. But at least it helps her to talk."

"It would help even more if she got on with her job. The woman's a menace. I wish we could discover that *she* put the body in the bath."

"Of course she didn't," said Paula. "Why should she?"

"Why shouldn't she? She had just as much opportunity as anybody else, and she was very keen to tell you that the doctor had said Mrs. Merton had taken too many pills."

"That doesn't prove anything," retorted Paula. "We are all longing to have it established that Mrs. Merton died by accident."

The telephone rang again. James moved towards it. Paula did a sort of dive over the back of the settee in order to get there first, gave her name, listened intently, and made frantic signs to James to keep away.

"Cathy?" he mouthed.

Paula covered the receiver. "Uncle Bill. I'll tell you later."

James sobered up at once, produced his crossword puzzle, and did not move nor speak until the conversation was over.

"Well?" he said, as Paula did not immediately speak.

"He's got rather a nice voice," she said. "Very plausible."

"But what did he say?"

"Nothing much. Sort of establishing himself as a nice guy. Hoped he wasn't disturbing me, thanked me for being a good friend and teacher to Cathy, nice to be in touch with the University of London again, might be coming over himself in the spring, hoped we would meet, and so on and so on."

"Didn't he even ask how she was?"

"Not directly. Rather anxious not to show any anxiety, I'd guess. I have a feeling that he might be just the slightest bit in awe of her. Or in awe of her money. She gave the impression that he was a prosperous and independent gentleman, but for all we know, she may be more or less keeping him. That's quite a thought," went on Paula excitedly. "Bill Prescott has been living off Cathy. Of course he won't be pleased if she finds her natural father. Maybe that's why he didn't want her to come."

"It's as good a theory as any," said James. "I'm rather suspicious of Bill Prescott, too. He sounds too good to be true. How do we know that he isn't Cathy's dad himself? He could be in league with the mother to put the blame on the runaway Frank Merton."

"I'd thought of that possibility," said Paula, "and I'm very much hoping for Cathy's sake that it doesn't turn out to be the truth."

"Why? I don't get that. He's cared for the child as a sort of stand-in father. Why should it upset her to discover he's the real thing?"

"Because she'd want to know why he never acknowledged her before. She would feel she'd been rejected by the person whom she loved best. It would be rather like those cases where a teenage girl has a baby, and in order to leave her free, the baby is brought up by the grandmother, believing the natural mother is its sister. I've always thought that must be a horrible shock, discovering that your older sister is really your mother. I don't think either you or I can quite realise what this sort of identity problem is. We are both firmly rooted in our own. We are lucky."

James thought this over and admitted that Paula was probably right. "In any case I don't see how Bill Prescott can be her father," he added, "because he really would have had to confess to her rather than let her set out on this pilgrimage. No, I prefer your theory, that he didn't want Cathy to switch her largesse to another."

"Or it may be," said Paula, yawning, "that he really is a nice guy, and doesn't want her to be hurt, and is pulling strings behind the scenes for her, to ensure that her search is successful. I can't think any more tonight. I've got to have some sleep. Are you staying here?"

"No. I've got to go home and feed Rosie."

"Goodnight, then, love."

"See you in the morning."

Paula was glad to be alone, but had she not been quite sure of being with James again in a few hours' time, there would have been no pleasant contentment in the temporary separation, but only a frightening glimpse of desolation and emptiness.

CHAPTER 5

"So we meet in the office," said James, "at about half-past twelve. If you haven't arrived by one, I shall come over to Bloomsbury Lodge to look for you, and since I'm a little squeamish about corpses, I shall be grateful if you will arrange not to be found in that condition."

"In other words, be careful. Of course I'll be careful, darling. And suppose you haven't turned up by one o'clock? Where shall I look for you?"

"You won't have to look for me because I shan't have moved from there. I shall conduct my researches into Dr. Arnold Frend by telephone, and spend the rest of the time marking essays."

"That's a relief," said Paula, "that you're not going to waste your whole morning."

It was also a relief, she thought as she walked through the gardens of Prince Regent Square, to know that James would come to look for her if necessary. Yesterday in complete innocence and ignorance she had found the dead body of an old woman; nobody in Bloomsbury Lodge could have had, at that time, any cause to wish her ill.

But today it was very different. Armed with Cathy's story and with her own suspicions, she was deliberately going to try to discover more about Mrs. Merton. The police had been over the ground and questioned everybody concerned. Paula's snooping around would certainly not be welcomed. But she had a legitimate reason for being there: Marjorie Gainsborough had invited her to coffee and a chat, and it was in the warden's flat that she was going to begin her researches.

At the enquiry desk she found a handsome and elegant Indian girl tidying up the register of bookings, handling the switchboard with great ease, and looking very much in charge.

At least one part of Bloomsbury Lodge is working efficiently, thought Paula, and wondered whether the girl, in spite of all this sleek competence that she was displaying, would be willing to take time off to gossip.

"I've come to see Mrs. Gainsborough," said Paula. "I think she is expecting me."

"Mrs. Gainsborough is in," said the girl. "Do you know the way?"

"I'm not quite sure. It's round here to the left, isn't it?"

"I will show you." The girl got up and accompanied Paula along a short corridor.

"Are you working here permanently?" Paula asked casually as they walked along.

The reply was very disconcerting. "I am a specialist in children's medicine researching at the institute. The new receptionist will arrive this afternoon."

"Where is Carlos, then?" asked Paula, feeling that she had made such a fool of herself that it hardly mattered what she said now.

"Carlos?"

"Yes. The boy who was here at the desk yesterday when I came to tea."

"I know nothing of Carlos. Here you are." She raised her hand in a beautiful flowing gesture and indicated a door on their right. "Go down the stairs beyond this door and turn left. There you will find Mrs. Gainsborough's apartment. The bell does not work very well, so you will have to ring several times. Or else you must use the door-knocker."

"Thank you," said Paula, feeling awkward and clumsy and still very much embarrassed by her mistake. But how could one possibly know that Marjorie had asked one of the residents to help her out on the desk? Why should she apologise? Nevertheless, she felt she ought to do so, and she turned back from the door, but the girl had already moved away, very swiftly and silently, and was halfway along the corridor leading to the foyer.

Paula pushed open the door. This part of the building was quite new to her, and she was struck at once by the contrast between the stairs down to the basement and those up to the attic. Subconsciously she had been expecting another lot of shabby uncarpeted steps, but as soon as she came through the door she had the impression of no longer being in Bloomsbury Lodge.

The stairs were carpeted in a rich plum colour, the walls were light and clean, and the apartment door, with its dark wood and its glass panel backed by a curtain, would not have disgraced any luxury apartment block.

Only the faulty bell was typical of the state of the rest of the building.

Paula pressed it twice, but nobody came to the door. This, however, might well have been due to the fact that there was a great deal of noise coming from behind it. The occupants of the flat seemed to be having a very loud argument.

Paula decided not to ring again, but stepped to the side, leaned against the wall with her face close to the edge of the door, and listened shamelessly. Presumably it was Marjorie and Joe, but she would not have recognised either of their voices. How little we know, she thought, of the domestic behaviour of people with whom we have only a slight acquaintance; and, indeed, of people whom we think we know quite well. Somehow one never expects one's friends and acquaintances to indulge in marital shouting matches.

The woman's voice was predominant. For a little while Paula could hear only a general hysterical shouting and could not distinguish many words.

Then she heard the man's voice say, so loudly that it made her jump and wonder whether he was actually about to leave the flat, "Will you shut up, you silly bitch! I tell you I've put the jewellery back. Of course it's not safe to keep it now."

"When did you put it back?"

The woman's voice, too, was now quite clear. Paula had the impression that a door inside the apartment had been opened and they were talking at each other through it, Joe trying to get away, Marjorie refusing to let him.

"Yesterday. Carlos took them to her."

"You fool! Then he knows, too."

"What should he know? What do you think he knows?"

This was said with a violence that startled the eavesdropper and was followed by sounds that might have been caused by a scuffle.

Paula began to wonder whether she ought to announce herself, or in some way raise an alarm to prevent murder being done.

Then suddenly the scuffling sounds stopped, and she listened closely, holding her breath, for the voices to come again.

This time it was the woman's voice, low but quite clear, and with a sort of resigned, almost contemptuous note in it that surprised Paula.

"You are a fool, Joe. You should have let me deal with this one. You'd better tell me all about it so that I know how to cover for you. When did you pick up the Bradshaw girl's pieces?"

The reply was such a mumble that Paula could not make out any words.

"And did Mrs. Merton actually see you take them?"

Again the answer was inaudible, but the question itself had set Paula's mind racing off along a new track: Marjorie Gainsborough, when she first learnt of Mrs. Merton's death, had reacted with horror and exclaimed, "Has Joe—" before she managed to control herself.

Perhaps she had been going to say, "Has Joe been involved?" or even, "Has Joe been arrested?"

The voices were becoming less and less audible. Presumably Marjorie was rehearsing her husband in the cover story. Paula decided that this was the moment to go upstairs again, out into the corridor, and then down to the Gainsboroughs' flat as if she were arriving for the first time. In fact she would have liked more than a minute or two to adjust her ideas about the Gainsboroughs and to prepare herself for a rather different sort of conversation with Marjorie than she had expected to have.

Should she return to the reception desk and say she hadn't been able to get an answer to the ring and ask the girl to call Mrs. Gainsborough on the internal phone? No. That would mean admitting that she had been at the door of the warden's flat. Although it was extraordinary, thought Paula as she stood undecided in the corridor, how quarrelling people would completely disregard the possibility of being overheard. Some years ago she had found herself in a similar situation, when invited to dinner with a couple whom she did not know very well. It was in an expensive block of flats, rather like the one where James lived, and she had stood outside the door, too embarrassed even to ring the bell, while her host and hostess yelled insults at each other inside the flat. On that occasion she had been rescued by the arrival of the other guest, and together they had played their expected parts, but the dinner had not been a success.

Whether the hosts had realised that they had been overheard, Paula never knew, since the acquaintance soon fizzled out. But in any case, that quarrel had consisted purely of personal abuse; it had not, as in the present case, concerned a theft, perhaps even a murder.

No, decided Paula, glancing along the corridor to the foyer, grateful that she was well out of sight of the reception desk, she must not let anybody know that she had already waited at the door of the flat. It would not only be unwise, it might be actually dangerous.

She managed to cram the small purse, which was all she was carrying, into her jacket pocket, leaving both hands free, and with one she pressed the bell and with the other banged the knocker.

Marjorie Gainsborough came to the door almost immediately, looking surprised and not too pleased by all this noise.

"I'm awfully sorry," said Paula rather breathlessly, "but they told me at the desk that your bell might not be working."

"My bell," repeated Marjorie as if she had never heard of such a thing, and then she seemed to take a grip on herself and invited Paula to come in. "Yes, the bell does keep going on and off," she said, "but with all the trouble we're having here at the moment . . ."

Here we go again, thought Paula; the "Troubles of Bloomsbury Lodge" tape was about to be played over again; it must be wearing rather thin, it was used so often by Marjorie to drown other sounds.

"Yes indeed," she said soothingly. "It must be awful for you, and you must be terribly busy. I won't stay long. . . . Yes, I'd love some coffee if it isn't too much trouble."

The offer had been made, but Marjorie still lingered in the door of the room into which Paula had been shown. There was no sign of Joe.

"I didn't know," babbled Paula, "whether I ought to ask the girl on the desk to phone down. She's a most terrifying young woman. How on earth did you persuade a high-powered medical lady to look after reception?"

"Is that what she said?" Marjorie actually smiled. "That she's a doctor? And you believed her? The little minx."

"You mean she isn't medically qualified?"

"Mira is the cousin of one of our cleaners. She's studying drama. It looks as if she might be a better actress than we thought. Make yourself comfortable. I won't be long."

Paula was annoyed with herself for being so gullible, but at the same time she could not help but feel grateful to the girl for putting Marjorie into a more amiable and relaxed mood. Marjorie's absence in the kitchen gave her the chance both to adjust her ideas and to look around her.

She had never been in the warden's flat before, and she found it even more surprising than to find a highly qualified physician on the reception desk. But this was real. This excellent furniture, some Victorian, some early twentieth century, was no mirage, and some of the pictures looked like originals of the Newlyn School.

Paula was examining the Wedgwood vases on the mantelpiece when Marjorie returned.

"They're nice, aren't they?" she said, putting down the tray. "They came to me when my mother died. And the Laura Knight landscape. And this coffee service. And a lot of other things."

But not this carpet, said Paula to herself, nor these curtains and chairs. These look more like Harrods, and quite recent, too. Had Marjorie inherited money as well? Or did the Gainsboroughs derive their comforts from some other source?

She took her coffee and admired the cup, wondering whether it would be safe to probe any further in this direction. Probably not. Marjorie would only repeat that she had inherited her goodies, and Paula would only have aroused suspicion and learnt nothing in return.

"I really came," she said after listening for some time to Marjorie's reminiscences of her childhood home in Devon, "to tell you that Mr. Prescott did ring me from Charlottesville last night. Thank you for giving him my number."

"Oh." Marjorie seemed to take a moment or two to adjust to the change of subject. "So Cathy Bradshaw did come to your flat?"

"No. She never turned up. I thought she just might. Isn't she here?"

"She didn't sleep here. Oh dear." Marjorie slid once more into her worried responsibility role. "I was sure she was with you. Just a minute. I'll check with Mira. Perhaps she's come back by now."

While Marjorie was telephoning, Paula looked out of the window. There was, of course, no view, but the area walls had been painted cream and were decorated by climbing plants in pots. Presumably Joe had gone out this way, through the door to the area and up the steps to the street. It was very convenient for the Gainsboroughs to be able to come and go without anybody in the main foyer of Bloomsbury Lodge knowing that they were doing so.

In fact, they had every reason to be very contented with their situation, and the last thing they would want would be any sort of scandal that deprived them of it. And if Joe had been adding to their resources by stealing residents' property—well, that would be another reason, in addition to laziness, for not troubling to repair the broken locks.

If it had not been for Paula's overhearings, she might have been coming to much the same conclusions as she was coming now, but she would have assumed Joe to be the villain and Marjorie to be the innocent, long-suffering wife. However, that conversation had shown them up in quite a different light. In their petty—or not so petty—thieving, Marjorie was an equal partner; maybe she was even the guiding intelligence, and her impatience with Joe would be not because of his criminality but because of his incompetence. On the other hand, she would draw the line at murder, and if Joe had killed Mrs. Merton because she caught him stealing, then—

"Oh dear." Marjorie sighed, putting down the telephone. "There's no sign of Cathy yet. And Carlos hasn't come back either. That wretched boy. Joe insisted on taking him, but I was against it from the first. These students are so unreliable. That's why we've got Mira on reception. She's turning out to be very good, and if I can only persuade her to stop practising her drama lessons while she's on duty, then I—"

Paula had great difficulty in interrupting and diverting Marjorie. Mrs. Gainsborough's domestic trials had been tedious enough, even when one believed them to be a genuine part of her character, but now that Paula felt sure they were a blind, she found them even more irritating than before. And not even very well performed. Marjorie must be under great strain. She was behaving almost like a caricature of her former self. Mira would have made a better job of it.

"I was dying to ask you on the phone last night," said Paula chattily, "how you found out that Mrs. Merton had taken an overdose, but I didn't like to say too much about it on the phone. You never know who might be listening. What did the doctor actually say? Could he tell by examining her how she had died?"

Let her think I'm a ghoulish gossip, said Paula to herself. If she can play a part, then so can I.

"Oh, Paula," exclaimed Marjorie, putting a hand to her mouth. "I've been awfully indiscreet. I ought not to have told you. We're not supposed to be talking about it."

"But it will all come out at the inquest."

"I know, but Joe says—"

So she's going to play the downtrodden wife now, thought Paula, so scared of her husband that she daren't say anything.

"Have you told the police that Cathy Bradshaw has disappeared?" she interrupted.

"Cathy hasn't disappeared. She spent the night out and just hasn't got back yet. It's not the first time that's happened. They are supposed to tell me, of course, if they are going to be away for a night, and the older ones always do. But these youngsters . . ."

Yet another tirade. Paula listened patiently, hoping to pick up some sort of clue, but Marjorie confined herself to generalities.

"What do the police think actually happened to Mrs. Merton?" Paula asked suddenly at the first possible opportunity, hoping that shock tactics might produce a reaction.

"I haven't the slightest idea," was the reproachful reply. "And I told you, Paula, we aren't supposed to be talking about it."

"But you must have formed some impression. Did they think it was an outside job?" persisted Paula, reluctant to give up completely, but not really expecting an answer.

To her surprise, Marjorie seemed quite willing to follow up this notion. Or perhaps it was not so surprising. From the point of view of the Gainsboroughs, it was much better that any suspicions concerning the death of Mrs. Merton should be directed away from Bloomsbury Lodge.

"They did ask if there was any access to the building apart from the main entrance," said Marjorie. "Of course we explained that we have a separate entrance here, but nobody else has a key and it is never left unlocked. And of course they wanted to know about the arrangements in case of fire."

"You mean climbing out on the roof and walking along beside the parapet?"

"It's a perfectly good escape route in emergency," said Marjorie.

"But could anybody get in that way?"

"If they can get out, they can get in."

"True enough," said Paula, forbearing to add that she personally would not like to sleep in a room where the window could easily be opened from outside, even if the possible intruder would have had to walk along the roof-top to reach it.

"So the police did consider the possibility that somebody had put Mrs. Merton in the bath," she said thoughtfully. "Why should anybody do that? She seems to have been a harmless old lady."

This was going too far. Marjorie had opened up only in order to try to widen the field of suspicion. She was certainly not going to speculate with Paula on possible motives for murder, and she now said, very sharply, that she could not possibly discuss such a matter.

"If you've got any sense, you won't talk about it either," she added. "It's none of your business, and it won't do you any good to stir up a lot of unpleasantness."

Here was a clear enough warning to keep out of it. Whether Marjorie was aware that she was speaking out of character or, rather, was speaking in her real and not her fake character, Paula did not know, but this was obviously the moment to withdraw.

"You'll let me know when Cathy gets back, won't you," she said, getting up.

"I'll tell Mira. She won't forget."

At the door another thought struck Paula. "Did the police find any relatives of Mrs. Merton? Is somebody coming to collect her things?"

Before Marjorie could repeat her little piece about not discussing the matter, Paula added, "I know you think I'm just being nosy, but damn it all, I did find the body and I did try to save her. I can't help feeling I'd like to know something about her. It's only natural."

"I believe somebody is coming this afternoon," said Marjorie. "I don't know any details. Joe spoke to him."

"That's good. It's horrible when somebody dies and no one cares at all. And it will save you the bother of dealing with the possessions," added Paula, giving Marjorie the chance of reverting to her role of anxious caretaker if she chose.

But the other woman had not even been listening. "Can you find your way out?" she asked, obviously thinking of nothing except getting rid of Paula.

"Yes, thanks. And thanks for the coffee."

The door shut behind her.

CHAPTER 6

Paula had no intention of departing from Bloomsbury Lodge just yet. She had intended in any case to have another look at Mrs. Merton's room if she could get into it, and her talk with Mrs. Gainsborough had very much strengthened her motive for going up to the attic floor.

First of all, she was worried about Cathy and was half hoping to find some sort of message, or at least some clue, as to where she had gone. And second, Marjorie's reaction to the suggestion that it might have been an "outside job" had set Paula's lively imagination working on the possibility of an intruder getting in through one of the windows. She glanced at her watch. There was at least an hour before James might begin to worry about her, but on the other hand she might have difficulty in getting upstairs and, even more, in getting out of the building unobserved. So it was best not to linger.

In the entrance hall, the Indian girl at the reception desk was very much occupied in presenting herself in some other role to a new arrival. She did not even glance in the direction of the staircase as Paula ran up to the first landing.

After that it was easy. Paula saw very few people at all, and nobody who might recognise her. The top of the house was completely deserted. It was a bright morning, and the sun's rays, shining through the dingy glass of the skylight, showed up the stained wallpaper on the attic stairs and the faults in the woodwork.

Paula looked first at the bathroom door, to which a notice was stuck which read NOT IN USE. She hesitated for a moment, then decided that the bathroom could not tell her anything new and that in any case she never wanted to see it again.

Cathy's room came next. The door was unlocked, the bed had not been slept in. The broken wicker chair was in exactly the same position as when Cathy had sat down in it.

Yesterday, Paula remembered, Cathy had been wearing the dark green trousers and the rather lighter green jacket that she wore for much of the time. In fact, Paula had only once seen her in anything else, and that was for the sherry party when she had worn a white lace blouse and a long black skirt. Either she was just not very interested in clothes or else she was determined never to give the impression of spending much money on them.

Paula looked into the clothes closet and opened the drawers of the rickety dressing-table. All evidence pointed to the fact that Cathy was still wearing the same things as yesterday and, presumably, still carrying the black shoulder bag. She had left Paula about nine o'clock the previous evening to meet Carlos, and it looked as if she had not returned to her room since then.

Were they still together? Where could they be? It was useless to speculate, but impossible to refrain from doing so. The happiest explanation was that they had gone back home with some friends or acquaintances after the show or the disco or whatever and were still sleeping off the night's amusements.

But what sort of friends or acquaintances would Cathy and Carlos, or either one of them, actually have in London? Paula told herself that she knew very little about Cathy's social life and nothing at all about Carlos. Presumably the Gainsboroughs would know something about the latter and would have some suggestions to make if Carlos did not return during the course of the day.

What about Cathy? She did not appear, as far as Paula could see, to take much part in student activities, nor did she seem to have made any particular friends as yet, either male or female. All her emotional energies were concentrated on the search for her father, and Carlos, Paula felt sure, was being singled out for favours only because he had been able to help her in this. There was no reason to suppose that she could be in any danger from him. Paula was determined to believe that Cathy was not, but it was not impossible that they might both be in some danger if they had been, not innocently employed, but trying to find out the truth about Mrs. Merton's death.

It was disappointing to find nothing about Cathy's room that was any help at all.

Paula half shut her eyes, trying to recall her first impressions of the room. A dark shadow, moving at the window, startled her until she realised that it was only a pigeon. She spoke to it, aloud, as she once more looked into the top drawer of the dressing-table, the drawer whose contents Cathy had upset onto the floor when she found the items of jewellery missing.

There were some personal letters, as Paula had already noticed when they retrieved the spillage, but to look at somebody's private correspondence was unforgivable. The situation, though worrying, did not warrant such measures. If anything had happened to Cathy —and even when framing the notion to herself, Paula employed this euphemism—then this would be a job for the investigating detective, and in such a situation obviously Paula would have to tell everything that Cathy had told her.

Hastily she shut the drawer. Time was passing, and she had not yet started on her other self-appointed task, which was to examine the fire-escape arrangements more closely. For this it would be better to be in Mrs. Merton's room, not Cathy's.

The other door was also unlocked. Was this just carelessness, or deliberate policy on the part of the Gainsboroughs? Again Paula told herself not to speculate, but to make haste, because while she might have been able to make some sort of excuse for being in Cathy's room, she could have no reason at all for being in Mrs. Merton's.

This room did not look so completely untouched. The suitcase that had been open on the floor when she came in and found Cathy was now closed and lying on the bed. Paula would have liked to look inside it; if Joe had done the packing, could he possibly have resisted that silver mirror and brush and comb? But to stop to investigate was to invite disaster. The main object was to have a closer look at the roof.

Paula moved to the window. It was open, and the sash moved up easily. Underneath it was an upright wooden chair.

Paula was just considering whether it was strong enough to be stood on when she heard footsteps on the attic stairs, heavy and deliberate steps, making no attempt to avoid the creaking floorboards. Certainly it was not Cathy. It was most likely Joe Gainsborough, going about his lawful business, and Paula was trapped.

Unless she got out of the window.

Paula had considered this possibility, but had not been very keen on it; she had hoped it would not be necessary for her own investigations. Now, however, was the moment to test the theory that one could cope with anything when there was sufficient emergency, and she hastily climbed up on the chair, sat on the window ledge, swung her legs over, and slid down the little way to the parapet without any difficulty at all.

It then occurred to her that Joe, if it was Joe, might be surprised to find the window wide open, and in coming to shut it he could glance out and see her. Better not stay here, but move farther along.

This Paula did, crabwise, keeping her face turned towards the slope of the roof tiles and supporting herself by touching them at frequent intervals. When she judged herself to be out of range of a casual glance, she crouched down in the space between the roof slope and the parapet to rest and think.

The height above ground level did not particularly worry her, but the sense of being at the same time so cut off and so exposed was not pleasant, and the thought that Joe, if it was Joe, might shut the window and prevent her getting back was more than unpleasant—it threatened to turn into panic.

The panic receded as Paula reasoned with herself. The narrow walkway on which she had taken refuge ran the full length of the buildings this side of Prince Regent Square. Somewhere along the row there must be another window that was open, or that she could open from the outside. Provided she took reasonable care, she would not come to any harm, and in the last resort there would be James coming to see where she had got to if she didn't turn up in the office by one o'clock.

So she might just as well make the best of her present uncomfortable and rather alarming position by finding out how easy—or how difficult—it actually was to get in at a window. How often, in academic work, did one set up a hypothesis and then attempt either to prove or refute it. Well, here she was, testing out the theory that somebody had got into Bloomsbury Lodge in an unorthodox manner and put Mrs. Merton—presumably unconscious, but surely not already dead—into the bath for the water to finish the job.

Paula had never meant to go to such lengths of experimentation, but she consoled herself with the thought that the best way to find out anything is by personal experience. Cautiously she straightened up from her crouching position and looked back at the window through which she had just climbed. The bottom sash had been pulled right down, but from where she stood she could see that the top one would be movable from outside. It would be awkward, but not intolerably difficult, to get back into the building.

Another source of comfort was that she now saw the iron handrail that ran from the side of the window to the parapet. It felt quite firm, and the tiles beneath the window were arranged to form narrow steps. In her hasty retreat from Mrs. Merton's room she had not noticed these conveniences, with which the two neighbouring windows, at least, appeared to be furnished as well.

Becoming more and more bold, she moved back towards Mrs. Merton's room to find out how much of it could be seen from outside.

The answer was, very little. The glass was too dirty, the light outside too glaring. Nor was it possible to hear anything from inside the room. The noise of the traffic down below, and the chattering of the starlings and sparrows protesting at the invasion of their space, drowned all sounds from within the building.

Was it safe to return? It was impossible to tell.

Suddenly Paula felt intolerably impatient at the thought of being here for another five or ten minutes or more, and to pass the time until she judged it safe to go back, she decided to explore further, still holding on to the intruder theory. Such an intruder would surely not have come from any of the other Bloomsbury Lodge windows, since that would be senseless, but must have come from the neighbouring house.

As far as Paula could judge, she was very near to the roof of that now, and as far as she could remember, this next-door house was divided into apartments for renting. Beyond it, at the corner of Prince Regent Square, was a small hotel.

Rented apartments and a hotel. In both there would be a lot of

coming and going. Hardly worth making enquiries, particularly as
she had no clear notion of whom she was enquiring about. It was
best not to think about that now, but to stick to the matter in hand,
which was to have a look at the nearest dormer window, which
would be the first of the attic windows in the apartment house.

Once again Paula began on her sideways walk, and this time she
progressed more quickly. It was extraordinary how one adapted oneself to circumstances. At this rate she would soon be in training for a
roof-tiler or a steeplejack.

What sort of proof that somebody else had passed this way might
she expect to find? Surely the police would have discovered any foot-
print in the dirt, or a tell-tale piece of cloth torn from a trouser leg.
Whatever idiotic pretensions made her feel that she might light upon
a clue where the proper authorities had failed?

The answer was that she knew a great deal that they did not know,
including a possible motive for the killing of Mrs. Merton. Two
possible motives, in fact.

There was Joe Gainsborough's thieving, and, from what she had
overheard, there was the fact that Mrs. Merton had caught him at it.
Then there was the other possibility, the one concerning Cathy. If
Mrs. Merton were indeed Cathy's grandmother, then she would be
able to tell the real Frank Merton from a fake one, which was more
than Cathy herself would be able to do. So if there were any impostor
in the offing—and surely this was a situation just made for impostors
—he would have a good motive for getting rid of Mrs. Merton.

The best evidence that somebody had come this way, thought
Paula as she negotiated the join with the next-door house, would be
the filthy condition in which the intruder would return to base. Her
own clothes were becoming plentifully stained with grime and bird
droppings, and her general appearance would take a lot of explaining
away.

For a moment or two her mind reverted to her own problem.
Perhaps she could clean up a bit in Cathy's room before she came
down to the front door of Bloomsbury Lodge. Or perhaps she was
going to end up by climbing into somebody's apartment and exiting
through the adjoining house. Anything was possible. She was beginning to regard her whole roof adventure with a sort of astonished

detachment, rather as if she were watching herself performing these antics in a film or television show.

But was anybody else watching them, too?

Not from Mrs. Merton's room, she now felt reasonably sure; but how about from down below, how about the windows of the apartment house, or those across the square?

The intruder would have had this problem, too. He would have been wise to make his base as near as possible to Mrs. Merton's window: the shorter the journey, the less risk of being seen.

Paula stopped again, supported herself by leaning against the roof tiles, and ventured to turn her head to look away from the building. Provided she did not actually look down, she was all right. What she could see was mostly the upper branches of the great plane trees, still plentifully burdened with leaves. It was extremely unlikely that anybody would be able to see her from the street below, or from the buildings the other side of Prince Regent Square.

The only danger lay in one of the other windows. How great was this risk? This was not a neighbourhood where bored or housebound people stared out at their neighbours from behind their window curtains. It was an area of short-term residents, students and tourists, where people were absorbed in their own affairs and did not even know their neighbours. At certain times of day, and particularly in the mornings, few of the people in these houses would be in at all.

What sort of person would be willing to take this risk, perhaps even delight in taking the risk? Paula imagined a character rather like Cathy herself: single-minded, persistent, brave to the point of being foolhardy. Overconfident perhaps. Egoistical? Possibly, but in that case he would not be like Cathy.

Paula was rather fond of trying to assess people's characters, but this was hardly the moment to indulge in the game. A couple of feet away from her was the first of the windows beyond Bloomsbury Lodge. It looked just the same; if anything, it had even more need of a new coat of paint. The bottom sash was down, the top one open a few inches.

And the curtains were drawn across, cheap faded pink curtains. Was the apartment empty? Was somebody sleeping late in there?

As Paula stood looking, she thought she saw the curtains move. It might perhaps have been a stirring by the breeze, although even high up here there was scarcely any movement of air on this fine October morning.

Had they moved? Was somebody standing there behind them, watching her, guessing what she was doing, what she was thinking?

For the second time since she had climbed out onto the roof, Paula felt panic strike again.

Hardly knowing what she was doing, taking risks that in a cooler frame of mind she would never have taken, she made her way back to Mrs. Merton's window, clung to the handrail with one hand and with the other manipulated the sashes until there was space enough to get through, and fell onto the floor, giving her ankle quite a severe jar.

For a minute or two she remained there, experiencing pain and relief in almost equal measure. Then she pulled herself up and looked around. The suitcase had gone from the bed. Presumably Joe had fetched it and would be holding it to give to whoever was collecting Mrs. Merton's things.

Or perhaps he had already handed it over. The thought that she might actually have caught a glimpse of this person, had she not been climbing on the roof, tormented Paula until she remembered that Marjorie had definitely said later this afternoon.

The time now was half-past twelve. James would soon be looking out for her and perhaps beginning to get anxious. Should she stop to try to get clean, or make a dash for it immediately?

Paula compromised by running into Cathy's room and using the clothes brush that she found there, sponging off the very worst of the bird droppings at Cathy's wash-basin, and combing her hair.

The result was just passable, provided she did not stop to speak to anybody who knew her. She hurried down the attic stairs, paused at the bottom of the flight to rest her ankle, and told herself that it would be much better to go steadily and calmly, as if she had a right to be there. Controlling herself as best she could, looking straight ahead and trying to give the impression of being very deep in thought, she came down the three lower flights of stairs and walked through the front door and out of the building.

The sight of the gardens raised her spirits. The other side of them was her office, James, and everyday life. It was now twenty minutes to one. She ought not to delay any longer, but there was just one more thing that she wanted to do. It wouldn't take long. Instead of walking across the road to the gardens, Paula turned left at the front entrance of Bloomsbury Lodge and walked the few yards to the next-door house.

CHAPTER 7

James was not actually waiting on the doorstep, as Paula had half expected, but pacing impatiently up and down their office, and he hardly allowed her time to visit the bathroom before hustling her out into the car.

Paula had rather hoped to spend a little time recuperating in the office. Her ankle was still sore, and she was longing to tell James about her exploits. But on second thought she decided that it was just as well to keep going. A comfortable chair, a cup of coffee, and a chat would probably reduce her appetite for adventure. She did, however, beg him to let her make her report before he made his. The morning had been traumatic, and she had simply got to talk about it.

So she gave him what she believed to be a light-hearted account of her visit to the Gainsboroughs and her subsequent activities, feeling better herself for the telling, and assuming that James would treat the affair in an equally casual manner and even be quite amused.

But he did not react in the way he usually did. For a little while he said nothing at all, and then, as they came out of the Central London traffic onto the approach to the motorway, he remarked in a rather strained voice, "Perhaps we ought to turn back. If there is really somebody lurking about on or near the roof of Bloomsbury Lodge, it might be better to be on the spot awaiting developments. It's not like you to run away in a panic," he added.

Paula had the impression that he was trying to speak lightly, but this last remark sounded more like a reproach. Something seemed to be not quite right between them, but she was still feeling more agitated than she realised: too agitated to read the danger signals.

"I didn't run away," she said indignantly. "I came because I knew you'd be waiting for me, and I thought you might be getting worried. Weren't you getting just a little worried, James?"

It was meant to sound teasingly affectionate, but instead of bringing them back into their normal state of ease with each other, it misfired completely.

"Of course I was worried." James executed a risky piece of passing. When they were once more back in the middle lane he went on, very irritably for so normally good-tempered a man, "Why do you think I join you in these murder hunts?"

Paula took a deep breath and did not immediately respond. She had recognised the warning light at last. Here it comes, she said to herself, the change between us. Of course it could not last for ever, that delicate balance of trust and detachment. One or the other of them was bound to become more demanding, to want more commitment.

At one time it had been she who was the more vulnerable, depending on him more than he depended on her, but now it was the other way round. Perhaps it was simply because women grew older more willingly, more confidently than men, having less of a power image to sustain, and often finding freedom and independence in their later years for the first time in their lives.

This was certainly not the sort of thing to say to James at this particular moment. He had now got into the fast lane again and was passing everything within sight.

Paula did not like fast driving. Her instinct was to yell at him to slow down and to add that they were in far more danger at this moment than they were likely to be in on her murder chase; but to say that would be to precipitate the threatened quarrel, and ninety-five miles an hour on the London-to-Oxford motorway was not the best occasion for it.

But if she didn't say anything, then James was going to go on driving like this, working off his own agitation, his own need of her and his own fears for her, because this was surely what it was all about, his fears for her when she put herself into dangerous situations.

She must say something, but it must not sound too careful, too rational, too well thought out, for he had sometimes accused her of always thinking before she felt, of intellectualising everything.

It would have to be direct and personal, nothing else would satisfy, but it was already too late for such a reaction. She ought to have yelled at him at once to slow down, as she sometimes did.

James was right, she did think too much.

She had now, at this critical moment, thought herself into a sort of paralysis of speech and will. Anything that she said or did would be the wrong thing.

Stop thinking so much. Just say what you feel. Anything, so long as it rings true.

"I'm absolutely dying for some coffee," she said. "Can't we stop at the next service station?"

"All right," snarled James. And then, a moment later, "As a matter of fact, we do need some petrol."

It was a sort of peace offering, or at any rate an offer of a truce until some more suitable circumstances arose.

The cafeteria was almost empty, and the coffee and buns quite tolerable. Paula stared at her table mat, which bore a picture of Windsor Castle, and said, "I was scared stiff on the roof. It would only take a broom handle, shoved out from a window, to topple you over into eternity. With very heavy odds against anybody seeing, and no proof at all that it had been done on purpose. I'd never have gone there if it hadn't been to get away from Joe. And if I hadn't known that you would come and look for me . . ."

James, stirring his coffee over a view of Oxford's dreaming spires, said, "I found out quite a lot about Arnold Frend. It's rather interesting. I'll tell you on the way. We won't go too fast."

This was the nearest either of them was going to get to saying "Sorry," but it was enough to establish a firm and friendly armistice and postpone the hour of reckoning to another occasion.

"Did anybody actually see you leave Bloomsbury Lodge?" asked James.

"Oh yes. There were several people in the hall. I didn't notice who. I just didn't want to know."

"And what about this house next door, where you think somebody was watching you from behind the attic window curtains?"

"It's split up into apartments and flatlets. You know the sort of thing. Each one has a bell and a name-plate. There's a janitor in the basement, slightly lame and rather deaf. He was hovering about the area steps when I came out and I asked him if there was a Frank Merton living there, since I couldn't see the name anywhere on the front door."

"Any luck?"

"Never heard of him, he said, but I did find out who was living in the attics. There are two apartments on each floor. Rosa Leaming is in one, and Mrs. D. L. Grosvenor in the other."

"Did you try them?"

"No reply from either bell. I'll try again when we get back to London, but I'm not very hopeful. It's the sort of place where people come and go a lot and don't trouble to change the name cards, and where people lend other people their apartments, or cram three or four students into the one room because they can't find anywhere else to live."

"Shifting population," said James.

"Yes, but not necessarily shifty. Talking of shifty, James, do you think I ought to tell the police about Joe Gainsborough? God knows I don't want to. I'm rather ashamed of the eavesdropping, but if you think, as a reasonably honest citizen . . ."

"I don't see why you should get involved. Let them find out for themselves. They're bound to do so sooner or later."

"Thanks. That's just what I wanted to hear. Do you want to go now? I'm ready."

In the car Paula said, "Thanks for stopping. I'm feeling much better now. Tell me about Dr. Arnold Frend."

"He was quite a well-known historian in his day," replied James, "but not the very tops, and nobody ever reads him now. In fact everybody I asked was surprised to hear that he was still alive. He must be ninety-four."

"Which makes him seventy-four when he was warden at Bloomsbury Lodge."

"Rather ancient for the job, which apparently he was never very good at anyway. He was unmarried and he wanted a convenient bachelor pad in Central London, but at the same time not to be bothered with any actual responsibility. It seems that he spent half his time in Oxford, and left a young protégé of his to look after Bloomsbury Lodge with the help of an elderly dragon of a lady receptionist. One of my informants remembers her and might even be able to track her down for us, if she's still alive. The place seems to have been just as bad then as it is now, except that they didn't even have a good cook. So I'm told."

"A young protégé," repeated Paula thoughtfully. "I wonder if history is repeating itself. I suppose you could say that Carlos is Joe Gainsborough's protégé. I wish I knew what part he is playing in the Merton affair. And I wish I knew where he was now. And Cathy. Sorry, James. Let's go back to Arnold Frend."

"Apparently he was exceedingly difficult to get rid of. Even when they did manage to oust him at last, there was a great outcry about this cruel treatment of an eminent scholar in his failing years. You know the sort of thing."

"Yes," said Paula, feeling slightly guilty and hoping that James would not pursue this aspect of the matter, because only last week she herself had signed a petition to allow a woman professor, now well into her dotage, to remain in a not dissimilar position to that which Dr. Frend had held.

"Academics," said James scornfully, "always stick together. Worse than lawyers or doctors. And they're much more out of touch with real life. They wouldn't last five minutes in the business world."

"I expect you're right," said Paula. And then she added meekly, since she knew that they were now on happy terms with each other again, "You inherited your money, didn't you, James? I wonder if you would have been any good at making it yourself."

"Hopeless," he said, laughing. "All right, so I've always been lucky and I've never deserved it. Can we take that point as settled for the time being, and return to Dr. Frend? He removed himself and the young protégé, name unknown, to the house in Clarendon Place where we are now going and let it be known that he was going to embark on a massive work entitled *The Decline and Fall of the British Empire*. This was presumably to comfort his bruised ego, because apparently it never got off the ground and he never wrote anything more at all. Not even the most pedestrian of contributions to one of the learned journals."

"That was twenty years ago," said Paula. "What has he been doing since then?"

"Mouldering away, becoming more and more gaga," replied James. "Like most of these superannuated scholars and writers. Like my own grandpa. You don't get many Bertrand Russells and E. M. Forsters. Most of the ninety-year-olds are suffering from senile dementia, and they are lucky if they've got enough money to pay somebody to put up with them."

"Money again." Paula sighed. "Clarendon Place. That will be one of those vast Victorian mansions. John Betjeman land. We'll have to go round the northern bypass."

Dr. Frend's house was much as they had imagined it, in a quiet cul-de-sac near to the University Parks. Take away the cars parked in the roadway, thought Paula, and the street would look just as it must have looked one hundred years ago, except that the dirty yellow brick walls would have been new and clean, and the softening surround of trees and shrubs would have been less luxuriant.

"What are we going to say?" asked James as he drew up behind a dilapidated Morris Minor.

Hastily they concocted a story. Two London University lecturers, happening to be in Oxford with time to spare, decided to call on Dr. Frend to convey to him the greetings of an old acquaintance of his.

"It sounds completely unconvincing," said Paula.

"It'll be good enough for whoever is looking after him," said James, "and if by chance we do get to see the old chap himself it won't matter what we say. The problem will be to stop him talking."

"Yes." Paula reached out and gripped his hand for a moment. "Thanks, love. Do you remember that old woman in Brighton?* You're so good at this sort of thing. Getting complete strangers to pour out their life story."

"Flattery will get you nowhere, madam," said James, but he was laughing all the same.

In front of the house was a high privet hedge broken at either end by green-painted wooden gates that opened onto a semicircular gravel drive. Beyond the left-hand gate was another, smaller gate labelled TRADESMEN'S ENTRANCE.

"That will suit us best, I think," said Paula, and pushed at it.

* See *The Mystery Lady.*

The front porch of the house was enormous and had a marked ecclesiastical flavour, with pointed Gothic windows enclosing red-and-yellow stained glass, and a long iron bell-pull.

"I can't even move it," said Paula. "There must be an electric bell somewhere. Or a door-knocker."

While they were searching, the heavy wooden door was pulled open from inside, and a girl's voice welcomed them.

"I saw you from the window. I guessed you'd come."

It was a clear and very happy voice, with its native American much more marked than previously. Cathy stood there against the background of stained glass and dark paint, eyes shining, cheeks glowing, an incongruously modern angel.

"I've found him!" she cried. "I've no doubt about it at all. Oh, Paula, isn't it wonderful! I feel as if I've come home."

And she flung her arms round Paula's neck and kissed her, and then hugged James, too, and pulled them into a huge, dimly lit hall, and assured them that they were not making too much noise and that they should make themselves at home.

"There's no one here but me. And the old man, of course. He's in bed upstairs. He's completely senile and doesn't notice anything. Dad's gone to London to collect my granny's things. We haven't had a chance to talk much yet, but he had to go and sort the rest of it out with the police and the Bloomsbury Lodge people, so I said I'd stay and look after Dr. Frend. And it doesn't matter that we've not yet had much talk because we've got all the rest of our lives. Oh, Paula" —and she flung her arms round her again—"it's you who did it. You got me going again when I'd somehow got stuck. Oh, Paula, I'm so happy. Except for poor Granny. If only . . ."

They had moved now into a cavernous room, overwhelming with its crimson drapes and dark Persian carpets and mahogany furniture, and Cathy stood for a moment at the bay window, looking out. Behind her back, James and Paula exchanged glances of puzzlement and alarm.

"If only I hadn't been so frightened and stupid," said Cathy, turning round, "I'd have had the chance to talk to Granny before she died. But of course I didn't know then who she was. She could have been anybody. A complete stranger. And there's no way in which I could have had anything to do with her death, Dad says. She had this heart condition and she sometimes took too many of her sedation tablets. He blames himself for letting her go to Bloomsbury Lodge, but she insisted on it. She was very obstinate, he says. So am I. I guess we're an obstinate sort of clan, we Mertons."

This is the moment, thought Paula, when I am expected to enter fully into Cathy's feelings. Most gladly would she have done so, if only she could have believed that all was well. But she could not help feeling that something was dreadfully wrong, and that Cathy's delight was an illusion that was doomed to break in bitter disappointment.

It would not only be cruel, it would also be pointless to try to modify her joy. Cathy was in no mood to listen to any doubts or counsels of caution. The only result would be that Paula herself would forfeit her confidence.

But pretence was so very difficult. It was like forcing oneself to offer congratulations when a friend made what one regarded as an unwise marriage.

"I'm so glad you are so happy," was all that Paula could bring herself to say. "I'm so glad that we found you here."

Of course this was not nearly enthusiastic enough to satisfy Cathy. James came to the rescue, as he so often did.

"What wonderful news. You must be over the moon. Paula has told me all about it. You don't mind, do you? We share everything, Paula and I. Including this terrific discovery."

Cathy turned to him with her most brilliant smile.

She thinks he is sincere, thought Paula rather sadly; he always sounds completely sincere. How does he do it? It isn't dishonesty. He really means it. He likes to say things that people want to hear, and that's no crime. He's quite recovered from our almost-quarrel in the car; he's fascinated by Cathy and her situation and is thoroughly enjoying himself; it is just not true that he doesn't want to come sleuthing with me and only does it to protect me. No, I am not going to change my whole way of living so that James doesn't have to worry about me, and . . .

". . . never known anything like it," James was saying to Cathy. "I feel as if I've walked right into the climax of a Victorian novel."

"So do I," said Paula, coming out of her own thoughts and making a great effort to play her part. "I'm absolutely stunned. You must tell us all about it, Cathy."

This seemed to be more acceptable. Cathy bubbled over, still turning more to James than to Paula, much to the latter's relief, since it gave her the opportunity to relax her features from the fixed expression of sympathetic delight and to let her thoughts wander again.

She was very conscious of James listening to Cathy, very anxious that Cathy should think well of him, and at the same time she was listening to Cathy's story and assessing it in the light of her own recent experiences.

"I came here with Carlos," Cathy was saying. "He's got a little old auto—I mean a beat-up old banger," she corrected herself, laughing, "and he drove me here last night when I told him I wanted to go to Oxford as soon as possible. We were going to stay at a hotel, but I thought, Let's at least find the house. You see"—and she turned to Paula—"Carlos had managed to find the address from where Mrs. Merton had booked in and it was the same as Dr. Frend, so I knew I was on the right track. She was his housekeeper. And my dad—"

"Just a minute," interrupted Paula, setting her own preoccupations aside and concentrating fully on what Cathy was saying. "You say this is where Mrs. Merton lived. Did you tell Carlos why you wanted to come here? Does he know that you believed Mrs. Merton to be your grandmother?"

"Oh yes. I told him everything. It was only fair. And he gets on fine with my father. They talk about the insides of motors, which doesn't interest me one little bit." She smiled happily. "That's how it all worked out. When we got here it was quite late—after midnight —but there were lights on upstairs and in the porch, and this guy came out into the garden—oh, Paula, you're going to love my dad!— and we got talking, and he was very interested in the old car—it seems he had one like it himself years ago and they are very seldom seen nowadays—and we were invited in, and of course we had to stay. And, Paula, you'd think my father, finding me after all these years like that, wouldn't have any time for Carlos at all, wouldn't you? But he did. That's what I liked so much. He didn't just ignore Carlos. He asked him about his position at Bloomsbury Lodge, and about the Gainsboroughs, and whether he'd talked to Mrs. Merton at all before she died."

"So he did know that his mother was dead?"

This time it was James who intervened. Paula would have said "Mrs. Merton," not "his mother," and again she admired the way that James slipped so easily into Cathy's version of events.

"He had only just heard," said Cathy. "He'd been away all day and had only just got back when we arrived. And the nurse who'd been sitting with the old man had only just gone."

"So he had only just learned that his mother had died?" James sounded very sympathetic, and again Paula mentally applauded him.

Cathy's face clouded for a moment. "Yes. Mr. Gainsborough spoke to him and told him it would be okay if he came to London this morning. He could see the police first and then collect Mrs. Merton's things in the afternoon. He offered to go last night. He was upset, of course, but he said it could have happened at any time. And then he was so excited about finding me . . ."

The smiles broke out once more.

Paula glanced at James. She felt sure that the same thought was in both their minds: Frank Merton lost a mother and gained a daughter, and benefited greatly from the exchange.

Cathy noticed that they were looking at each other. "I ought to offer you some tea," she said.

"That would be very welcome," said Paula, scenting a chance to be alone with James for a minute or two, "and if we could use the bathroom . . ."

Cathy jumped up at once and began to show off the house. Had Paula not felt so convinced that the girl was under a dangerous illusion, she would have been amused at Cathy's attempts to adapt herself to her surroundings and play the hostess in this very outdated English setting. The staircase was wide, with low treads, thickly carpeted in dark red, and the carved banisters were highly polished.

"When I was a child," commented Paula as they followed Cathy up, "I used to be taken by my grandparents to visit their friend who was housekeeper in a place like this, and I always longed to slide down the banisters."

"You can do it now if you like," said Cathy, laughing. "Nobody will know. The old man won't care. I'll go and have a look at him now. Just a moment."

She pushed at a door that was slightly ajar and returned to say that Dr. Frend was still asleep. He slept most of the time, and a nurse came in several times a day to attend to him. Granny had looked after him at nights—she'd been housekeeper here for years—oh, hadn't she explained that?—and Dad lived with her and helped. They moved from Wilsham to Oxford when the old cottages were pulled down.

"He didn't get in touch all these years," went on Cathy, "because my mother told him not to and he thought it would be best for me to forget all about him and grow up as an all-American girl, but of course I couldn't forget. Anyway, I must leave you in peace now and go and make that tea. We'll use the best china. It's like something out of the Victoria and Albert Museum. Here's the bathroom. That's a museum piece, too." She laughed again, said, "Don't be long," and ran off down the staircase, humming happily to herself.

The bathroom was indeed very quaint, with both bath and lavatory pan surrounded in solid dark wood, and a chain with a porcelain handle to flush the latter.

"It's even more of a period piece than my grandfather's," was James's comment.

"And better plumbing than Bloomsbury Lodge," was Paula's.

They lingered on the first-floor landing.

"Frank Merton," murmured James. "It all sounds very convincing."

"She's only his word for it that he's Mrs. Merton's son. He could be some sort of manservant here. Or an acquaintance of the old man. He could be anything. Cathy would never know. Mrs. Merton is dead, and Dr. Frend is senile."

"But there's that photograph," James reminded her. "If that's genuine, then this man must at least have a strong physical resemblance to the real Frank Merton."

"Twenty years ago. People change."

"He's making very free with Dr. Frend's home."

"That's true," said Paula thoughtfully. "This young protégé that Dr. Frend had—what do you think, James?"

"That's just what I am thinking. He would be the right age. But there is no reason why the young protégé should not be the real Frank Merton. Suppose he returned from America, went straight to Bloomsbury Lodge—probably he already knew Dr. Frend, might have been one of his students—and settled in there, eventually taking over all Dr. Frend's affairs and maybe helping himself as well. He brings his mother in as housekeeper, and they do very nicely so long as the old man is alive. But when the old man dies—"

"Perhaps he's already dead. Perhaps it's a corpse in there."

"Shall we look?" James moved towards the bedroom door.

Paula pulled him back. "Ssh. I can hear Cathy downstairs. We'll have to go or she'll get suspicious. We must act as if we believe she's found the real Frank Merton, and we must try to stay here until he gets back."

"That won't be difficult. She's dying to show him to us."

They moved to the stairs. Cathy was at the foot, calling up to them.

"We've been exploring the house," said James, very much at ease. "It's like my grandfather's. G. E. Goff. You may have read some of his books."

"Of course I have. I never knew you were related to him, Dr. Goff. Isn't that lovely?"

Even Cathy was momentarily diverted by this mention of the famous novelist, and by the time they returned to her own affairs they were all three talking together like the closest of friends.

CHAPTER 8

"So Bill Prescott really did write to your father," said Paula, care-fully replacing an extremely ornate blue-and-gold teacup in its sau-cer. "You told me that he loved to arrange delightful surprises."

"That's right," agreed Cathy. "When he saw I was determined to come over alone, he fixed it all. He hadn't heard anything of Dad for years, so he only had the old Wilsham address, where the cottages have been pulled down, but the Post Office was very clever and the letter got here in the end."

"Have you read it?" asked James.

"I have, and there's no doubt that it's Uncle Bill's handwriting, and his style." Cathy beamed at them both. "I'm not all that daft," she went on, addressing Paula. "This is the most important thing in my life, and I wasn't going to accept any old fraud just because I was so keen to find my father. There's no wishful thinking about it. Even you will have to be convinced, Paula, when you hear the whole story."

"You're convincing me more and more every minute," said Paula truthfully. "What did Bill Prescott actually write?"

"Oh, something quite cryptic. I guess that's the way they used to talk to each other. I forget the exact words. Dad is holding on to the letter himself. It was like a clue in a treasure hunt. 'Bloomsbury Lodge, October 3, arriving from Charlottesville, somebody you'll find it worthwhile to get to know.' Something along those lines."

James and Paula digested this.

"Of course Dad had guessed it would be me," continued Cathy, "and he talked it over with his mother. He was rather nervous about the meeting—well, that's natural, isn't it? He didn't know what my mother had told me about him, he didn't think it would be very kindly, and he was afraid that I could be hostile. So his mother—

Mrs. Merton—suggested that it might be better if she came by herself to check me out. It would be easier for a woman, she said, to make a casual acquaintance with another woman in a place like Bloomsbury Lodge, but it was Dad's idea that she should say she was doing research in the British Museum. I guess that was just their joke, she being a housekeeper. And when she'd got to know me and made sure that I really did want to find my father for good reasons, then she'd fix the great reunion scene. Just like Uncle Bill wanted."

Cathy paused.

"But it didn't work out that way," prompted Paula.

"No, because I behaved so stupidly. If only I'd known . . . but it would have made no difference to her dying in that way. Even if we'd got to know each other, she'd still have taken too many tablets when she felt this pain coming on and would have collapsed somewhere or other. It might have been somewhere even worse than in the bathroom. It can't be my fault that she died, can it, Paula?"

"In no way, in no possible way," cried Paula warmly.

James joined in the reassurances. "If anybody is to blame at all," he added, "it's Bill Prescott for not going about the business in a straightforward manner. Beautiful surprises are all right if they come off, but they are very liable to go wrong. Have you been in touch with Charlottesville yet? Does he know about Mrs. Merton's death?"

"No," replied Cathy. "Dad said he would call him this evening when he got back from London. Or maybe tomorrow. He didn't actually say so, but I don't think he's very pleased with Uncle Bill. At least, he hasn't said much about him. It's rather as if he's avoiding the subject, but of course, as I said, we haven't had a chance to talk very much just yet because Carlos was with us last night and this morning till they went off together in the old car."

"Carlos was driving him to London?" said Paula, with a quick glance at James.

"That's right," replied Cathy. "It seemed silly to take two cars, and Dad is getting the train back. He ought to be here soon." She got up to move towards the window, and at that moment there came a loud knocking at the front door.

"It can't be him," said Cathy, "because he's got his key. It must be the nurse for Dr. Frend. I won't be long. Help yourselves to more tea."

She shut the door behind her, and they heard voices in the hall.

James spread his hands in an eloquent gesture and looked questioningly at Paula.

"I still think there's something very wrong somewhere," she said stubbornly. "Okay, so there was a letter from Bill Prescott setting up the scene. By now he ought to have had an ecstatic phone call from Cathy, and maybe a somewhat less enthusiastic one from his old pal. But nothing has happened as far as he knows, and he's getting worried. Hence his telephone calls."

"I can quite see that Cathy's father could be embarrassed about meeting her," said James, "and that he would be willing to let the old lady spy out the land first."

"I'll buy all that," said Paula, "but what I can't take is Mrs. Merton's death just at this moment."

"The inquest," began James.

"Of course the inquest is going to show that she'd taken too many pills and got confused and drowned herself in the bath. He would never risk such a story if it didn't agree with the facts."

"Here, wait a minute!" cried James. "Aren't you assuming rather a lot? We have no proof that Frank Merton had anything to do with his mother's death, but we do know for certain that Joe Gainsborough had a motive. And what about Carlos? Don't you find it very interesting that he and Frank got on so well from the first time they met? I'd like to know whether it really was the first time. Suppose they were in it together. The inside man and the outside man. Together they could fix anything."

"That's very true," said Paula slowly. "I must say I was rather surprised when Cathy said that Carlos had driven Frank up to London in his old banger. I'm sure there's a Mercedes, or at any rate a Rover, locked up in that garage. I've been uneasy about Carlos all along. It seemed to me that Cathy was putting far too much trust in him."

"As she now is in Frank."

"She's so terribly defenceless. Just a minute."

Paula got up and went to open the door. "I thought I heard something," she said as she returned to her chair, "but there's no sign of anybody. It looks as if there might be a bit of a crisis upstairs, but we'll sit it out, won't we, whatever happens. Or do you want to go?"

She looked at James appealingly, and he burst out laughing. "Of course I don't want to go. I'm well and truly hooked on the Merton mystery. It's just that when you—no," he interrupted himself firmly. "We are not going to discuss that now. We will make a special date for it. A candlelit dinner with a carefully chosen menu. And on the agenda a frank and full discussion of how far I should be obliged to be a helpless spectator of the Perils of Paula. Okay?"

"Okay, darling. Very, very okay." Paula stretched out a hand.

"Then let's get back to Cathy. Do you think Mrs. Merton ought to have announced herself at once to Cathy instead of waiting a day or two?"

"No," said Paula. "I think that's quite plausible. After all, we know nothing about Mrs. Merton. Maybe she wasn't that keen on discovering a long-lost grandchild from America. She might well have wanted to see what sort of a girl she was before claiming her as her own. I think, in her place, I'd have wanted to do that, too."

James agreed. "And if, as we suspect, both the Mertons have been living off Dr. Frend for years, there may well be things that they would prefer to keep hidden from a bright young daughter from across the Atlantic."

"Exactly. But it doesn't seem to be worrying Frank now."

"Meaning," said James, "that he trusts himself to handle Cathy but he didn't trust the old lady to? So he killed the old lady for fear she would give the game away? His own mother?"

"I don't know," cried Paula in despair. "I just don't believe in the official version of the death. And I don't trust Frank Merton. Why won't he talk to Cathy about his old pal Bill Prescott? Wouldn't you do so, in his place?"

"Of course I would," said James promptly. "I'd be cursing him heartily for making such a balls-up of everything and I'd be on the phone to him at once, whatever hour of the day or night. You're right there, Paula. That is very suspicious indeed. If Frank doesn't want to contact Bill or even to talk about him, it could be because Bill would know at once that he is not the real Frank."

"But Mrs. Merton would have known that, too. Why didn't she tell Cathy?"

"Let me think of a reason," said James. "Ah. I've got one. Frank and Mrs. Merton are working together, scrounging off Dr. Frend. If the old man dies they may lose their source of income. Along comes the letter from Bill Prescott, and they see the chance to live off Cathy Bradshaw instead. But maybe, after having seen the girl, the old woman turns soft and has to be got out of the way. How about that?"

"It sounds possible," said Paula. "If you're impersonating someone, it's much safer if nobody else knows about it at all. He must be sufficiently like the real Frank Merton to take everybody else in. With Mrs. Merton out of the way, and assuming that Carlos is not involved, then Frank's only danger lies across the Atlantic."

"Six hours' flight away. Is he going to pop over and murder Bill, too, do you think?"

"I think," said Paula firmly, "that I had better telephone Bill Prescott at the very first opportunity and tell him everything, and hope that he will come over immediately and sort it all out."

"If you do that," said James, looking rather alarmed, "for God's sake don't let Cathy know about it or even suspect. You could be on dangerous ground. There's been one death already, and—"

He broke off as the door opened. In their excitement they had been forgetting to speak softly, and Paula, seeing Cathy's face, was afraid that she might have overheard something. But all Cathy said was, "Dr. Frend seems to be getting weaker. The nurse thinks we ought to call the doctor."

"Then perhaps we'd better go," said Paula, "now that we know you are all right."

"Oh, don't go." Cathy sounded genuinely disappointed. "I do so want you to meet my father."

"But he won't want to be bothered with visitors when he gets back," said Paula. "Could we come another time? Or perhaps meet in London before the inquest."

Cathy appeared to be considering this suggestion seriously, and Paula, watching her closely, began to wonder whether she was, after all, beginning to lose some of her happy confidence. Could it be that something of Paula's own scepticism had communicated itself to her? Or that, now that Frank Merton was no longer actually present, the euphoria had begun to fade and doubts to creep in?

Paula would have liked to believe this, but she felt that it was more likely Cathy was simply worried about Dr. Frend.

"I hope he will be all right," Paula murmured politely.

"Oh, I do hope so," said Cathy. "I do wish you'd stay until the doctor comes."

There was no refusing this direct appeal, particularly since it coincided with their own inclinations.

When Cathy left the room again to let in the doctor, James whispered, "Is the gilt wearing off?"

"I think so," Paula whispered back. "I think it's occurred to her that it was a bit tough on her, being left alone here with a dying man. Do ask her why she didn't go to London with her father. You'll do it better than me."

James nodded. When Cathy returned he said, "It must be a relief to you to have the doctor here. It's a pity you didn't go up to London, too, and leave the medical people in charge."

"I didn't want to go," said Cathy, scenting a criticism of her father. "I love this house. It feels like home."

"But will it still be your home," said James gently, "if Dr. Frend does not recover?"

"I—I don't rightly know," replied Cathy, looking rather bewildered. "I guess he's left the house to Dad. I'm sure he's left it to Dad," she amended.

"So you will stay here? You would like to live in Oxford?"

"I don't know." She sounded even more uncertain. "I've not really thought about it."

She looked very different from the wildly happy girl who had first opened the door to them; she looked like somebody coming, confusedly and painfully, out of a dream.

"Let's hope that Dr. Frend will recover," said Paula kindly. She was glad, for Cathy's sake, that the process of adjusting to reality had begun, but wished she could be of more help. "In any case," she went on, "I hope this doesn't mean you are going to abandon your work. That would be a great pity after you've made such a good start for your M.A."

Cathy grasped eagerly at this reference to her studies. It's like a lifeline, thought Paula, in the midst of all the uncertainty in which she finds herself. For whatever Cathy's feelings about England, it was in fact a strange country to her; and her father—if indeed he was her father—was a stranger; and to be left in charge in this vast house with no company except a senile and sick old man would have been a heavy responsibility for any girl, whether or not she was a stranger in the land.

After a few more remarks about the English department at college, Cathy began to look more like herself again, and she was once more beginning to talk about her father, when they were interrupted by a youngish woman in a blue nurse's uniform who came into the room without knocking and hurried over to Cathy in an agitated manner.

"You must come at once," she said. "Please hurry. It's urgent. Doctor says so, Miss—I don't know your name."

And she ran out of the room again, followed by Cathy, who now looked thoroughly alarmed, and who turned back at the door to look appealingly at Paula.

"We're not going to go away," said Paula. "Whatever happens, we are going to stay here until your father gets back. Come and fetch us if you think we can help at all."

When the door had closed, she turned to James and said, "She shouldn't be left to cope with this."

"No, it's not fair on her," he agreed.

"It's nearly six," went on Paula. "Why is Frank away so long? He only had to collect a suitcase at Bloomsbury Lodge, and even if he just missed a train there are lots of others which don't take much more than an hour."

"Perhaps he's been arrested," said James.

But Paula did not smile. "We've got to do something about this. I'm going to phone Marjorie Gainsborough and find out what time he left." She was hunting for the number as she spoke. "I ought really to have phoned her before to tell her that Cathy is all right."

Mrs. Gainsborough switched on the worried responsibility tape as soon as she recognised the caller, and it was with difficulty that Paula got her message through.

Marjorie then switched from being distraught to being suspicious. "What are you doing in Oxford? What's Cathy doing in Oxford?" she demanded, as if it were in some way a crime to be visiting an ancient university city.

"Visiting friends," said Paula abruptly. The thought of explaining the whole situation to somebody who would only listen to two words at a time was unendurable, and she began to wish she had never made the call. "Did Mr. Merton come to fetch the suitcase?" she went on hurriedly in a slight pause for breath at the other end.

"What suitcase?"

With her free hand Paula made gestures of desperation to James, who shook his head and looked sympathetic.

"Mrs. Merton's," said Paula. "You said somebody was going to collect it this afternoon. You told me this morning that Joe had arranged it."

"I don't know what Joe arranged. You'd better ask Mira. She's looking after the residents' luggage now. And why on earth Cathy didn't tell me that—"

Paula interrupted the flow. "Can you put me through to Mira now?"

"I can't put you through from here. You'll have to ring the other number. Is Cathy with you?"

"Yes, but she's busy."

Paula realised that this sounded absurd. James was making signs at her to ring off.

Suddenly she had an inspiration. If Marjorie refused to know anything about the dead woman's suitcase, at least she must be interested in the return to Bloomsbury Lodge of her errant desk clerk.

"What time did Carlos get back?" she asked.

That would at any rate establish that Frank had got to London, since he and Carlos had been driving together.

"Carlos isn't back," said Marjorie, "and if he knows what's good for him he never will be. The boy was a terrible mistake, Paula. Even Joe has had to admit it now. He took him in without references, you know, just on the strength of a letter from an old pal of his at Columbia. I never trust these old pals, and he's been a nuisance all the time, always wanting time off to study, and—"

Paula would have liked to protest that this was unfair. From what she had seen, and had heard from Cathy, Carlos worked hard at both his studies and his job, but there was no point in trying to argue now. The news that he had not returned to Bloomsbury Lodge was disturbing, but at least she had gained some information from her telephone call.

"We think now," Marjorie was saying, "that his disappearance is most likely connected with—with things that have been disappearing from residents' rooms lately, and—"

James, seeing Paula's look of amazement, came and sat on the arm of her chair.

"I've got to go, Marjorie. Sorry. Goodbye," said Paula hurriedly. "Would you believe it?" She turned to James in great indignation. "Carlos hasn't come back yet—and they're going to blame him for Joe's stealing."

"Calm down, sweetie. They won't get away with it. If it comes to the crunch, you tell the police what you overheard."

"But where on earth can he be? And Frank, too?"

"Perhaps they had an accident. It was an unreliable old car."

"We'd have heard about it ages ago."

They stared at each other.

"Isn't there another number you can ring?" asked James.

"Yes. Reception desk. Let's try. There's this role-playing drama student answering the switchboard. Don't be put off by her."

It seemed a long time before there was any reply from the reception desk at Bloomsbury Lodge, and Paula was just about to give up when Cathy burst into the room crying, "I can't handle this thing—I just can't!" She snatched the telephone from Paula, cutting off the call. "I've got to get Dad. He's got to come home."

James tried to soothe her. "We're trying to locate him now. We were through to Bloomsbury Lodge. Let me try again while you tell us what's happened."

Cathy was persuaded to ease her frantic clutch of the telephone. She sat down on the arm of a chair and seemed to be trying to get herself under control.

"He's dead," she said at last. "And the doctor says he ought not to be. Oh, what am I to do?"

CHAPTER 9

Neither James nor Paula could make much sense out of Cathy's first explanations. The only sentence that was clear to them was "Where did he get the whisky?" It was a relief when the nurse came back into the room, followed by a tall, thin man who seemed equally relieved to see them, introduced himself as Dr. Allen, heard their names, told the nurse to attend to Cathy, and briefly explained.

"I can't sign a death warrant until I have spoken to somebody in authority. There seems to have been some neglect of my instructions, with serious consequences. Do you know where Dr. Frend's house-keeper is? Or her son?"

"Mrs. Merton has had an accident," replied Paula. "Didn't Miss Bradshaw explain?"

All eyes turned to Cathy, who was now leaning back in an arm-chair, silent and terribly pale, looking around her in a dazed manner.

She has come down to reality with much too sharp a jolt, thought Paula. "I'd better explain, Dr. Allen," she went on. "Miss Bradshaw has had some rather bad shocks." And she hastily described the finding of Mrs. Merton's body, and added cautiously that Cathy Bradshaw had reason to suppose that she was related to the Mertons and had, in fact, come to England to try to trace them.

"Mr. Merton has gone to London to collect Mrs. Merton's belongings," concluded Paula. "He ought to be returning any moment now. We were trying to find out what time he left."

"I see. Well, perhaps you could try again," said the doctor. "I don't mind waiting for a little while. Meanwhile, perhaps we could make Miss Bradshaw more comfortable."

Cathy did indeed appear to be in a state of shock. After a brief consultation it was decided that sedation was the answer, and while Dr. Allen and the nurse took her upstairs, James got through once

again to Bloomsbury Lodge, telling Paula as he dialled the number
that he was going to be very firm with Mira.

"Cut out the drama," he said sharply into the telephone. "This is
really important. There's been a sudden death and I need to contact
Mr. Frank Merton urgently. What time did he—"

He broke off and for a moment or two was speechless. Paula,
watching him closely, could not help but smile at the expression on
his face.

"I've got the wrong woman," he mouthed, putting his hand over
the phone. "It's not Mira. It's a lady professor from Edinburgh,
staying at Bloomsbury Lodge. There's nobody else on the desk. She
just picked up the phone."

He removed his hand and began to apologise.

Paula was tugging at his arm. "Are you quite sure? That girl's a
wonderful mimic. Let me talk to her."

James pulled away, continuing his apologies, and finally rung off.
"Oh, do shut up, Paula. It was Helen McClintock. I tell you. I've
met her. God knows what she must think of me."

Paula was still not convinced and wanted to try again. The telephone rang while they were fighting over it, and Paula grabbed it
first.

"Yes, Cathy Bradshaw is here, but she is not very well at the
moment. Dr. Allen is with her. Who is that speaking?"

She listened for a little while and then said, "So we can expect you
in just over one hour's time. All right. I'll ask Dr. Allen if he will
wait. Yes, we'll look after Cathy."

"Frank Merton?" said James.

"Yes, from a call-box at Paddington Station. Just about to get on
the Oxford train. Was very delayed by the car breaking down this
morning. Worried that he'd had to leave Cathy alone for so long. Dr.
Allen is to wait. He won't mind. He gets big fees for looking after Dr.
Frend and will be hoping for a legacy. We're going to meet him at
last, James. We can't possibly leave here now."

"Leave here? Walk out of the theatre when the curtain's going to
go up at last? What's the matter with you, Paula? Just because I get
worried sometimes when you do daft things—"

"Candlelit dinner agenda," Paula reminded him.

"Which reminds me that I'm hungry," said James plaintively. "Do you think we could go and raid the kitchen? I don't see why not, do you? After all, the owner of this house is now dead, and our hostess, if you can call her that, is now asleep. Or do you think we ought to wait until Frank Merton gets here?"

"I don't know the etiquette for such a situation," said Paula, "but I'm sure Cathy wouldn't mind. I'll go and forage while you talk to Dr. Allen. You might learn something from him. Do the man-to-man stuff. He doesn't think much of women. You can tell that by the way he talks to the nurse and the way he treated Cathy."

She was placing the coffee-cups back on the tray as she spoke. "I only hope they've got some plainer crockery," she said. "I'm terrified of breaking these things."

The kitchen was on a similar scale to the rest of the house and appeared to contain all its original fittings: cooking-range, scrubbed deal tables, red floor tiles, and wooden dressers displaying a fine variety of willow-pattern plates and dishes. It was like a museum piece, and Paula wondered how even the most devoted housekeeper could possibly work in here, until she saw that leading off the kitchen was a rather smaller room, presumably the Victorian scullery, which was fitted up with modern equipment and every possible labour-saving device.

It did not take her long to find the means to make sandwiches, but she deliberately refrained from hurrying, in order to give James time to talk to Dr. Allen. If the doctor was indeed doubtful about the death but eager to benefit from it, then James would be just the right person to convey a sympathetic understanding of the dilemma. Paula had every confidence in James's ability to ferret out information from the sort of person who was impressed by wealth and social status. He had less success with older men who had had to struggle, and with women with feminist inclinations.

But that category includes myself, thought Paula, smiling to herself. And I am changing much more than I realised. Even during these last few hours there has been a change.

Those alarming moments on the motorway seemed a long time and a long way away. Danger had flared up; it could so easily have been the beginning of the end of their relationship. But the will to keep it alive had prevailed, and it was useless to speculate which one of them had played the major part in the truce.

Candlelit dinner, said Paula to herself as she cut slices of cheese. That is never going to take place. Not for the purpose of discussing my sleuthing, at any rate. But they would refer to it now and then, a little private memory, as they did to the Hampstead Register Office at the age of sixty.

It's the things we talk about but don't do, she thought suddenly, that bind us even more than the things we did. T. S. Eliot's "passage which we did not take." She must share this thought with James, if ever they had the chance to talk at leisure again.

She had left open the scullery door, and that of the main kitchen, in the hope of hearing some sounds from the front part of the house, and she was not disappointed. A murmur of voices and the click of a door closing told her that the nurse had left. She finished making the sandwiches, found a bowl of fruit, thought for a moment, and then, because she had always been very fond of blue willow pattern, took down some of the cups and saucers from the dresser.

There was still well over half an hour to go before Frank Merton could be expected to arrive. I'll give James another five minutes on his own with the doctor, decided Paula, before I take the tray in. Meanwhile I'll go up to that bathroom again.

The door of the main sitting-room was closed. Paula could hear voices but did not linger. Upstairs there was deathly quiet. Indeed, Paula reminded herself, there was death in the house. Behind the door to her left. Should she go in? No one would hear. In any case, she had always the excuse that she had come up to have a look at Cathy and had mistaken the room.

The heavy, white-painted door moved silently over the thick carpet. The curtains were drawn across and the room was dim. When her eyes had adjusted themselves, Paula could make out the shape of a small four-poster bed. She moved closer. The occupant of the bed had been a big man. His head was big, too. There was a plentiful surround of white hair against the pillow, and the eyes were closed, the skin bleached-looking.

The old man might have been sleeping, not dead. How much he could have told us, thought Paula, and then corrected herself: No, he could not have told anything worth hearing if he had been senile and confused.

But perhaps he had not been. Suppose he had been quite clear in mind and liable to be talkative if he got the chance. Suppose that somebody had been afraid he might say more than he ought?

Paula turned to the bedside table, where there stood a jug half full of water and another with fruit juice. A glass with a little orange juice left at the bottom stood beside them. Paula bent closer, careful not to touch anything, and sniffed at the glass.

Whisky. It was unmistakable. And here was the empty bottle, pushed behind the water jug. Cathy, before she became incoherent, had said something about forbidden whisky.

So that was it. The fatal mixture of alcohol and drugs. No wonder the doctor was treading very carefully.

Paula stood for a moment or two staring at the table and thinking hard. If Dr. Frend had been deliberately given alcohol, in the full knowledge that it would have fatal consequences, would that be murder? Surely not. It would be the old man's responsibility. Suicide rather than murder. He could hardly drink whisky without knowing he was doing so. But suppose he was so confused that he did not know what he was drinking? Confused because he was senile, or because of the drugs he was being given.

That would make it easier, if he had in any case a taste for whisky, to ensure that he would drink the fatal dose. But if he was confused in mind, then he was unlikely to present any threat to somebody who didn't want him to talk.

"If only you could tell me," murmured Paula aloud. "Oh, what a tale you would have to tell."

For if anybody had a close knowledge of the Mertons, it was surely this old man, whose life had been so closely bound up with them for many years.

It could not, it simply could not be a coincidence that he had died at the very moment when the heiress daughter arrived from America. But if he had been given the forbidden drink in order to ensure his silence, there was certainly going to be no proof of it; no more, Paula felt sure, than there was going to be any proof that the death of Mrs. Merton had been intended.

The situation was full of possibilities, full of opportunities for the people concerned to twist it whichever way they wished.

Who would benefit by the death of Dr. Frend? His heirs, of course. The Mertons? Or had he, in spite of all pressures, cheated them at the end by leaving his fortune to some distant relative or to charity? And what about the doctor? Frank had taken trouble, even in that brief phone call from Paddington Station, to say that the doctor was expecting a legacy. So was all this business about possible negligence just an act? Or was Frank simply trying to widen the net of suspicion?

If only she could find out what the old man's mental condition had really been. So much seemed to depend on the answer to that question. She had only Cathy's word for it that Dr. Frend was completely senile, and Cathy was only echoing Frank.

A senile old man could pose no threat. Hold on to that, said Paula to herself. But a mind even partially alert could present a danger. Was there no way to find out whether Dr. Frend had been capable of communicating with other people in a rational manner during the period preceding his death?

Mrs. Merton would presumably have known, but she herself was dead. And the doctor would know; but could one trust the doctor to admit the truth if it didn't suit his own purposes? What about the nurses? They would very likely just follow the doctor, but there was a faint hope there, if only one could get hold of them.

As her mind worried away at this possibility, Paula looked around the room. In the light that came through the gap in the curtains she could see the wardrobe and the tallboy, both dark mahogany; a small table, some upright chairs, and some bookshelves. Opposite the end of the bed was a television set, but of course she could not know whether the old man ever watched any programmes, nor with what degree of intelligence he viewed them. The radio standing on the bedside table might be more conclusive evidence that he was aware of what was going on around him, but there again it might only mean that a restless confusion could be soothed by soft music, or that the nurse had the radio for her own comfort.

What else? Very reluctant to leave the room without learning anything more about its owner, Paula tugged at one of the heavy window curtains to admit more light and noticed, for the first time, lying on the floor between the bed and the window, a folded newspaper. She picked it up, too eager to be cautious, and found it was the day's *Times,* folded over to reveal the crossword puzzle. About half the clues had been filled in, in red.

Paula knelt down, felt along the carpet, and with great triumph retrieved a red ball-point pen.

A loud explosion from a motor-cycle in the road outside made her jump up guiltily, with racing heart. She controlled herself sufficiently to replace the window curtain to its former position, and then hurried from the room.

Out on the landing she hesitated for a moment. She would have liked to make sure that Cathy was quietly resting, but it was too risky. The important thing now was to smuggle this newspaper and pen out of the house. Unfortunately she had nothing with her in which to conceal it, only the little purse tucked in her jacket pocket.

There was really no reason why she should not run out of the house with the paper and pen in her hand, leave the front door ajar for her return, and leave her findings in James's car. No reason at all except that she was so anxious about having picked up what could be an important clue that she did not want to risk any encounter until it was somewhere safe.

She returned to the kitchen, still holding the copy of *The Times,* and hunted in the dresser drawers for a paper or plastic carrier bag. After a short search, she found one with a picture of a well-known bookshop stamped on it, inserted the copy of *The Times* and the ball-point pen, added her own purse and, for good measure, a couple of apples from the fruit bowl, and held the carrier bag casually in her left hand while she pushed open the door of the main sitting-room with her right.

"I've made some sandwiches," she said brightly. "Would you like to have them now?"

James and Dr. Allen looked up from what appeared to have been an earnest conversation.

"I'm so sorry," said Paula. "Did I interrupt something?"

Both men got to their feet, protesting that she had not disturbed them at all and that they would be grateful for the refreshments.

"The tray's on the kitchen-table," said Paula to James, "and there's beer and fruit juice in the fridge. May I have the car-keys, James? I've left my tissues in the car and I can't stop sneezing. Hay fever maybe."

He produced the car keys at once, and Paula ran off before the doctor could finish saying that there was a packet of tissues in the bathroom. When she got back to the sitting-room, she found that James and Dr. Allen were talking about their cars, and the three of them continued to pursue this harmless topic of conversation while they ate and drank and waited for Frank Merton to return.

CHAPTER 10

Paula felt Frank Merton's fascination from the very first moment she saw him. He was a striking-looking man in his mid-forties, with the same dark hair and deep blue eyes as Cathy, and the same ready smile. As far as Paula could remember from the photograph that Cathy had taken from Mrs. Merton's room, the young man on the right could be Frank. And he might well be Cathy's father, but family likenesses are odd, elusive things, and one could not accept a certain physical resemblance as a firm proof of blood relationship.

Paula had to keep reminding herself that this man could well be an impersonator, might even be a murderer, and that she must hold tight to her own theories and her own suspicions of him and not allow herself to be dazzled.

For Frank Merton did indeed dominate the room. Even James, who had more than his fair share of good looks and was quite an impressive personality, seemed overshadowed by the newcomer.

"Where's Cathy?" was his first question after the briefest of greetings and introductions.

Very right and proper, thought Paula, that he should think first of her.

Dr. Allen explained. "Please don't wake her if she's still asleep," he added. "She was very distressed and needs the rest."

"I won't upset her," said Frank. "She's much too precious to me."

It was said without any affectation or exaggeration and sounded completely convincing. Either he was a very good actor or else he was just what he seemed. After he had left the room, Paula longed to ask the doctor if he had known that Frank Merton had a long-lost daughter in America, but decided that this was not the right moment. In any case, James would surely have mentioned it when he was talking to Dr. Allen.

There was a short silence after Frank had left the room. Then James stood up. "If you don't want anything more to eat," he said, glancing first at the doctor and then at Paula, "I'll take this tray out to the kitchen."

"I'll bring the fruit bowl," said Paula, taking the hint and getting up, too.

"Any luck with the doctor?" she whispered while they were placing their respective burdens on the kitchen table.

"Not much. Very cautious. Tell you later. What d'you think of him?"

"Frank Merton? I could go for him."

"Careful, Paula."

"Jealous, darling?"

"Not jealous," said James seriously. "Just worried for you. But I'm not allowed to be, am I?"

"No need to worry," said Paula. "I'm not nearly glamorous enough for Frank, and Cathy—"

"Is much too young for me," finished James. "As a matter of fact, I wasn't thinking of amorous adventures at all."

No, thought Paula, you are thinking of my personal safety, as you were on the motorway. But this time, reading his thoughts, she felt no impatience but only a longing to reassure him.

"I'll be very careful," she said. "Anyway, I can't come to any harm while you're here. I think we ought to go back now."

Only when they were once more in the sitting-room did Paula remember that she had not seized the opportunity to tell James about *The Times* crossword puzzle. But it would have taken too much explaining, and it would be much better for them not to be seen conferring in private, even though Frank Merton must know that this was not just a social visit.

He can't be pleased to find us here, thought Paula, particularly if Dr. Frend was meant to die; but he's handling it extremely well, treating us as Cathy's friends, thanking us warmly for being so concerned about her.

He will go first to Cathy's room, her thoughts ran on, and make sure she is not awake. And then he will go into Dr. Frend's room, to check that all is in order there. Will he know that there was a copy of today's *Times*, with half the crossword clues filled in? Will it be the first thing he looks for, in order to remove it so that nobody will ever know Dr. Frend was clear in mind?

Stop thinking about it, Paula said to herself. There is certainly going to be no police investigation, not even an inquest, in this case. The doctor is going to write out a death certificate, after a little private talk with Frank; a funeral will be arranged, an obituary notice will appear in *The Times*, and Arnold Frend will soon be forgotten except by the occasional scholar who chances to look at one of his books.

Whether or not he had been capable of independent decision and action at the time of his death would be of interest to nobody. It was only in Paula's consciousness that the question assumed such great proportions.

And perhaps in the consciousness of Frank Merton.

It was as if they were all waiting for him; waiting for him to stage-manage this scene, the aftermath of the death of a once eminent scholar.

Paula, who had been leaning back in her chair, staring unseeing at the reproduction of Landseer's *Monarch of the Glen* that hung over the mantelpiece, shifted her position and glanced up to see James looking at her with an expression of such affectionate concern that she nearly cried out. But the presence of Dr. Allen, although he was now seemingly absorbed in the local evening paper, hindered her, and all she could do was smile at James instead.

How could she reassure him, when she felt so apprehensive herself?

"I do wish he'd hurry up," said Dr. Allen, putting down his newspaper. "I've got other patients to visit. I've already spent far too much time on this case."

You don't talk like that when Frank Merton is actually here, said Paula to herself, silently addressing the doctor. I believe you're rather scared of him, too.

James spoke soothingly. "He'll be down in a minute. You'll soon be able to get away."

Paula, partly to avoid encountering another such look from James, partly because she felt restless, got up and pretended to study the books in the shelves next to the door. James and Dr. Allen were talking in a desultory manner.

The door opened. Paula, standing only a couple of feet away, looked up as Frank entered. Perhaps, in moving instinctively nearer to the door, she had sought to provoke this brief but close exchange of glances. He knows I distrust him, she thought; he knows we are enemies. He will want to find out how much I actually know. He can easily find out that I've been upstairs.

"I'm sorry to keep you waiting," said Frank as he came farther into the room. "I thought I might as well pay my respects to the dead while I was up there. Dr. Frend looks very peaceful. It's been a good, long life. Hardly an occasion for mourning, but I'll miss him nevertheless."

"Mr. Merton," said Dr. Allen, getting to his feet, "I should like to speak with you privately."

James got up, too. "It's high time we were going. We had no intention of intruding for so long, but as Cathy seemed so anxious that we should stay, we felt that—"

Paula interrupted him. When James was nervous and agitated, which she knew he was at this moment, he would go on apologising for too long. She could not endure that Frank Merton should observe this weakness of his. She was aching to be gone so that she and James could relax together and be themselves again.

"Goodbye," she said to Frank, disgusted by the falseness in her own voice. "Now that I know Cathy is safe with you I shan't worry about her any more. I hope I've been able to be of some use to her, and I hope she will soon return to her studies, because she looks to be doing very well."

"I'll make sure she gets down to work," said Frank, "as soon as she's recovered from these upsets. But I'm going to keep her here with me for the time being. There's a good train service and she can come up and down to London for her lectures. Bloomsbury Lodge is no place for her. I can't think why Prescott ever let her go there. Nor why he thought up this idiotic way of bringing us together after all these years—but then he always was an incurable romantic."

It sounded totally convincing. If I remain any longer in this man's company, Paula said to herself, then I shall not only be in danger of finding him more and more fascinating, but I shall be in danger of believing everything he says. No wonder Cathy had been so euphoric, with such an act directed at her.

"I had trained myself to put both the child and her mother completely out of my mind," went on Frank, "when I set out to try to build up a life for myself in England again. A clean break seemed the best thing. So I wasn't entirely pleased to get Prescott's letter, though I couldn't help being curious. And my mother, of course, was even more so."

He paused, but nobody spoke. There was something mesmerising about those brilliant blue eyes.

"But I mustn't keep you," he went on, "nor Dr. Allen, who has been delayed quite long enough already. You have a car here?"

Paula and James found themselves shepherded towards the front door, and for one bad moment Paula thought that Frank was going to accompany them to James's Rover and find an excuse to search inside it for that missing copy of *The Times,* which she had simply dropped onto the back seat, with no attempt at concealment.

But he came no further than the doorstep, and said pleasantly as they parted, "I ought to have taken my own car this morning, but I hate driving in London, and since this boy that Cathy picked up was going up in his old banger . . . I wonder if he ever got it going again. I left him somewhere near Henley and had quite a long walk to the nearest bus stop. After that, well, it was tedious, to say the least, and caused a long delay. Goodbye, Dr. Glenning. Call me here if you want to know how Cathy is, and very many thanks for your good care of her."

"Oh, that's all right," said Paula awkwardly. "No trouble. Glad to help."

James pulled her away.

In the car she said, "That man's a hypnotist. He causes one to babble."

"You're right, love. I don't think either of us has cut a very imposing figure, as they say."

"And he'll have that poor sap of a doctor exactly where he wants him," said Paula. "If there's anything suspicious about Dr. Frend's death, it's certainly never going to be uncovered."

They came out onto the main road out of the city.

"Motorway or scenic route?" asked James.

"It's getting too dark for scenery," said Paula, and then quickly added, "But I've just thought of something—d'you mind stopping a minute, James?"

He pulled onto the side of the road, blocking the driveway of a house rather similar to that of Dr. Frend. Traffic coming out of Oxford city centre sped past. After the fine day a light rain was falling.

It felt good to be out in the real world again, and Paula said so.

"If Carlos's car broke down somewhere near Henley, as Frank said it did, then they would have been going on the old road, not the motorway. That's odd, isn't it?"

"Not necessarily," said James. "If the car was as unreliable as it seems to have been, he might not have trusted it on the motorway."

"That's possible, I suppose. I wonder how long it took him to get it going again."

"A hell of a long time, since he hadn't got back to Bloomsbury Lodge when we phoned."

"And Marjorie is using him as a scapegoat for their misdeeds. It's very convenient for her and Joe, isn't it, Carlos being away so long."

James groaned. "Please, darling, I cannot bear any more suspected crimes. If you are going to suggest that the Gainsboroughs somehow contrived for Carlos to disappear—"

"I didn't mean that. I just wondered if Carlos has his own reasons for keeping away. Maybe he's doing some investigation on his own."

"Or maybe it was he who put Mrs. Merton in the bath, and Frank has now paid him off and he's on his way back to New York. What do you want us to do now, Paula? Personally I should love to go straight home to my place and feed the cat and have a decent meal and return to civilised life. But if you feel you've absolutely got to pootle around in the wet and the dark in the side roads near Henley looking for a broken-down old Ford, then—"

"The sacrifices you do make for me," interrupted Paula. "No, love, it's senseless. Can I have a bath when we get back?"

"Dozens, if you like."

When they were on the motorway Paula fell asleep, and James

drove as quickly as he wanted, but it was steadily and contentedly, not working off any hang-ups at all.

By mutual consent they did not talk about the Merton affair until Rosie had been fed, Paula had had her bath, and they were dispatching the chicken casserole that James's cleaning woman had left for him. Then Paula explained why she had wanted to smuggle the copy of the newspaper out of Dr. Frend's house, and James reported on his tête-à-tête with Dr. Allen.

"It wasn't very productive," he said. "He's only been treating Dr. Frend for the last six months and has seen very little of Frank, but he seems to have been quite friendly with Mrs. Merton. I had the impression that both he and she were very interested in how much money the old man would leave."

"That sounds more than likely," said Paula. "But did you gather that Frank wasn't actually living in Clarendon Place?"

"Oh no. He seems to have been living there more or less permanently for some time. It doesn't necessarily follow that he and Mrs. Merton were related to each other."

"And it doesn't necessarily follow," said Paula thoughtfully, "that he is a good and worthy citizen even if he really is Cathy's father."

"Sorry," said James, rearranging the black cat more comfortably on his lap. "I don't quite get it."

"What I mean"—Paula lit another cigarette—"is that we have rather been assuming that the real Frank Merton is okay, not a bad lot at all, and that if somebody really has been contriving a series of 'accidental' deaths in the hope of financial gain, then that man must be an impersonator and not the real Frank."

"Yes, I think we rather have," said James slowly. "Either he's really Frank, and good, or not Frank, and bad. We must have both been dazzled by those gorgeous Irish eyes. I'm sure those two are blood relations. They've both got that Svengali look about them. Extraordinary ability to make people believe what they want believed."

"So let's take it as read," said Paula, refusing to be sidetracked, "that this man really is Frank Merton, son of the late Mrs. Merton and one-time buddy of Bill Prescott of Charlottesville, Virginia, who came back to England twenty years ago without any money and without a job.

"He'd got an old mother in a village near Oxford and he might have had some connections with Bloomsbury Lodge. At any rate, he went there. Suppose he stayed on, helping Dr. Frend, who was lazy and inefficient and came completely under Frank's control. Frank gets his mother in to housekeep, and between them they make a very good living out of the old man, live in great style, and do anything they like, more or less. Doesn't that sound a plausible scenario?"

"Very convincing indeed," agreed James.

"How, then, will they feel," continued Paula, now well launched upon her lecturing manner, "when the letter arrives from Bill Prescott?"

"Very intrigued indeed." James stemmed the flow by getting in this quick answer to what had been a purely rhetorical question. "At the same time not unreservedly delighted. Long-lost daughter from America might turn out to be an asset, particularly as she has riches to dispense, but she might equally well be an awful nuisance, upsetting the scene completely."

"In any case she won't be asking them for money," said Paula, "because it's clear that she's coming over with the idea of giving away and not of taking. And Frank and Mrs. M. are very fond of money. That's for sure."

James laughed. "You are learning at long last that most people are capable of almost anything if they scent financial gain. Yes, they are very fond of money, which means that they will always want more than they've got. So they are afraid Cathy might disturb their nice little arrangements, but they also want to meet her, just in case."

"But perhaps we might allow them a little natural curiosity? After all, one's own daughter, one's own grandchild."

"By all means," replied James, "allow them any feelings that you like to attribute to them. They want to meet Cathy, and they start off by going along with Bill Prescott's devious plan. So far we have nothing inconsistent with Frank being himself but not being a villain. Now comes Mrs. Merton's death."

They both pondered this for a while. James played with the cat and Paula smoked another cigarette.

"It probably really was an accident," she said at last.

"According to Dr. Allen, who's been attending Mrs. Merton as well as the old man," said James, "she did have a tendency to overdose herself when she got attacks of palpitations."

"It's accidental then. Or else Joe did her in . . . but let's stick to the Mertons for the moment. The Bloomsbury Lodge people got in touch with Frank, and meanwhile Cathy came to Oxford in search of him. Driven by Carlos. The great reunion scene took place in Clarendon Place, and Cathy was over the moon."

"Cut at that point," put in James, "and everything is innocently explained."

"Except Carlos disappearing."

"We didn't know about it then."

"But we do now." Paula got up from the table and began to wander about the spacious living-room. James's dressing-gown trailed on the floor around her. First she opened the inlaid rosewood box that stood on the coffee table, found it empty, and shut it again. Then she ran her fingers along the mantelpiece, and after that began to open and shut the drawers of the sideboard.

"If you are checking on whether Mrs. Hudson cleans the place properly," said James severely, "the answer is that she does. If you have run out of cigarettes and are looking for more, there are some in the study. Top left-hand drawer of my desk."

Paula stopped her wanderings, sat down again, smiled rather guiltily, and said, "I'll try to do without. If you'll do something for me."

"Anything, any time, no need to bargain," said James expansively.

"It's nothing very demanding. Just to telephone Bloomsbury Lodge again and see if Carlos has got back. I don't feel I can endure another conversation with either Marjorie or Mira."

"I should think it would be the night porter by this time," commented James as he drew the telephone towards him.

It was indeed a male voice. James signed to Paula to listen in on the extension in the study. She did so, and was very tempted to join in the conversation when she recognised the voice as that of Joe Gainsborough.

"I wonder if you can help me," James was saying politely. "I've just got back from Oxford, where I've been visiting Miss Bradshaw, one of your residents who is staying there for the weekend. She is a student at the college where I teach, and I promised her to enquire about a young man who works part-time as a reception clerk. She called him Carlos. I'm afraid I don't know his other name."

There was a moment's silence, and then Joe's voice said, "I'm sorry, I can't help you. Carlos is no longer employed here."

"Then could you tell me where I might be able to find him? Miss Bradshaw was most anxious—"

"I can't help you." The voice was no longer making any pretence at courtesy. "You'd better get in touch with the police."

"Missing persons division, you mean?" said James.

"Criminal investigation," snapped Joe before cutting off the call.

Paula replaced the receiver on the telephone extension and returned to the living-room, tripping over James's dressing-gown and looking very indignant.

"That sneaky hypocrite!" she exclaimed. "He's going to scapegoat the boy. I ought to have told the police myself. I'd better call Inspector Beal now."

"Darling, darling!" cried James, saving her from falling headlong as she took an impulsive step. "Can't we leave it alone for a while? If they do by any chance catch up with Carlos and he spends the night in a police cell, it won't do him any harm. He's young and strong. And personally I don't believe for a moment that the Gainsboroughs have set the police on his trail. The last thing they want is for him to be found. He's only of use to them as a suspected missing person. They don't want him turning up. Too much risk that he'll not only prove his own innocence, he might even prove them guilty. For all we know, dear Paula, Carlos actually *knows* that they're guilty. Maybe he's even been blackmailing them. Maybe anything. Let him look after himself. I'm sure he's capable of it. You've done quite enough championing of people for the time being. And I've certainly had enough. It's been a very long day."

Paula could not deny it. Carlos was no helpless innocent, and certainly not as emotionally vulnerable as Cathy. His continued absence was very likely nothing to do with the Bloomsbury Lodge situation at all. His car had broken down; probably it needed a spare part that could not be obtained for a day or two.

"If I were him," said James after advancing these arguments, "I'd find myself somewhere to stay overnight until the garage had fixed the car."

Paula agreed readily with this commonsense explanation. She was too tired to argue any more, but the events of the day continued their kaleidoscopic workings in her mind and wove themselves into her dreams.

CHAPTER 11

It was, however, not Paula, but James who spoilt the leisurely Sunday-morning ritual of newspapers and coffee and hot rolls, by opening up the subject of Cathy Bradshaw again.

"Are you going to phone Bill Prescott? You said you wanted to."

Paula was reading one of the more lurid Sunday papers and did not look up. "Just a minute," she muttered. "I've got to find out whether the vicar really was guilty of—"

James caught hold of the paper and they read it together.

"How very disappointing," said Paula sadly when they had finished. "It all amounts to precisely nothing."

"It always does," said James. "The real villains are much too clever to get their stories into the papers. Frank Merton, for example. Don't you think you ought to make that call to Charlottesville?"

"It's too early," objected Paula, glancing at her watch. "It'll only be four in the morning there."

"All right, then. Make it at lunch-time."

Paula did so, but was relieved to get no reply.

She tried to explain to James why she had suddenly lost all desire to talk to Cathy's Uncle Bill, but since she did not fully understand her own reluctance, she was not very successful in her explanation. At any rate, James for once did not seem to understand.

"You aren't thinking of abandoning the Bradshaw enquiry, are you?" he asked.

"Wouldn't you be pleased if I did? I thought that was what you wanted."

The words came out almost peevishly. It was she who was now provoking a quarrel, and James who was keeping his cool.

"It seems a pity not to see it through," he said mildly. "Is it because you're scared of Frank? Or afraid that you might fall for him?"

"Neither," snapped Paula, while admitting to herself that it was probably a bit of both. "Anyway, it was you who were telling me yesterday to take care. Don't you remember?"

This was terrible. What on earth was the matter with her, attacking James like this? What had become of all that lovely harmony of the previous day, after they had made their truce?

James had done nothing to break it; it was all her own doing.

"I'm sorry, love," she said. "I think I must be suffering from a surfeit of Mertons. It might be a good idea if I spent the rest of the weekend catching up with some work."

"A very good idea. I shall do the same."

"See you tomorrow, then," said Paula as she kissed him goodbye. "I'll make dinner this time. And thanks for everything."

It really was best that they should be apart, she said to herself, and they really did need to catch up their own lives, both of them. It would be hopeless if we were married, her thoughts ran on as she strolled for a few minutes on Hampstead Heath before the short walk home; I'd get these moods and ruin it all.

James, sitting down at his desk to complete the book review that he had started on two days ago, found an old newspaper lying on his typewriter. It was the one that Paula had abstracted from Dr. Frend's room after his death. He pondered over it for a moment, wondering whether it was as important as she seemed to think. Maybe. At any rate, it was worth keeping safe.

As he put it in the middle drawer of the desk, on top of a pile of typing paper, he wondered whether she had left it behind on purpose or just forgotten it. Perhaps it was a Freudian slip, a little half-conscious gesture indicating that she would like him to take over the unravelling of the Merton business now.

She need not worry. He had no intention of distancing himself from it. Not now that Paula's curiosity had got her into a position where she could pose quite a threat to several quite unscrupulous people. Her evidence would be enough to make life very uncomfortable for the Gainsboroughs, but luckily they did not yet know it. Then there was Frank Merton. Without having quite Paula's conviction that he was the villain of the piece, James felt sure that he was very devious indeed.

It would be a very good thing if Paula were to lie low for a few days—at least until after the inquest on Mrs. Merton.

James wound a sheet of paper into the typewriter. On the whole he was rather pleased with the success of his own policy. By urging Paula on, by making no more protests about her putting herself in danger, he had actually managed to put her off the whole business for the time being.

Paula was quite unaware that she was the subject of such calculations. Work was her well-tried and sure refuge from emotional upsets, and she settled down with determined concentration to marking essays and drafting lecture notes. She even tidied up the flat, so that all chairs were free of piles of papers, and all the books lying on the floor had been replaced on the shelves.

Then, still feeling full of energy, she drove over to her sister's and stayed to look after the children while the parents, unexpectedly granted a free evening, took themselves to the cinema.

By Monday afternoon Paula had worked herself out of the irritable mood and was looking forward to spending the evening with James. Her interest in the Bradshaw-Merton affair was reviving, but it probably would not have led to any action had not Cathy turned up at the afternoon seminar. Paula hadn't expected to see her, but there she was, punctual, pretty as ever, and apparently completely recovered from the events of the last few days. She made some useful contributions to the discussion, and when the meeting broke up she stayed behind to talk to Paula.

It was like a replay of the previous meeting, except that Cathy, instead of being nervous and tense, was bright and confident.

"Everything's absolutely fine," she said, "and I just don't know how to thank you for all your help. Dad wants to thank you, too. Properly. Have you got time to talk, Paula? Can we go and have tea somewhere?"

"Bloomsbury Lodge?" suggested Paula, not meaning it seriously.

"Sure. Why not? I've paid my rent up to the end of the month. We might as well have some more of that lovely cake. That is, if you don't mind going there after what has happened," added Cathy doubtfully.

"I don't mind if you don't."

"To tell the truth," confessed Cathy as they once again walked through the gardens together, "I'm not so keen to go up to the top by myself. I don't believe in ghosts, but there's a kind of scary feel about it. Do you know what I mean? I don't feel that way at all about Dr. Frend," she went on. "But then that was different. It was quite natural. Dr. Allen has found out that one of the nurses had been smuggling in whisky against his instructions, and Dr. Frend didn't understand enough to know that he ought not to drink it. Dr. Allen says it's not our fault at all, and he's signed the death certificate and there's no need for any enquiry. But of course there's people to be informed and the funeral to arrange and a lot of legal business, and Dad is attending to that now. He'll tell me all about it when I get home this evening. I'm going to catch the eight-fifteen. . . ."

Cathy chattered happily on, very much at ease. Paula had a vivid memory of her on that previous walk, only a few days ago, stopping beside the little Jubilee memorial tree, and talking about her dream coming true.

It had looked, at the hour of Dr. Frend's death, as if that dream might be shattered, but it now seemed that Frank Merton had done an excellent repair job. I am not going to start feeling concerned for her again, Paula told herself. But of course she knew that she already was, that her detachment of yesterday was only self-deception, and that her discovery with Cathy of Mrs. Merton's body had created between them a bond that could not be broken, or could be broken only by the discovery of the truth.

Did Cathy really suspect nothing? Or was there, perhaps in her very brightness, a certain element of pretence?

They came in at the front entrance of Bloomsbury Lodge, just as they had done before. But there was no dark brooding boy to greet them at the reception desk, only a plump middle-aged woman who looked at them incuriously.

"Yes, tea is being served now," she said in answer to Cathy's question, and returned to her knitting.

"The new receptionist, I suppose," commented Paula as they

moved into the lounge, where an elderly man looked up from his conversation with an elderly woman and smiled at Cathy.

She greeted him back. "The nice old guy I sat next to at meals once or twice," she explained to Paula as they helped themselves at the serving table. "That'll be his wife. He said she was going to join him for a day or two before they went home to Cornwall."

Cathy now sounded rather less cheerful. She is remembering, thought Paula, the day before Mrs. Merton died, the day when she rejected her own grandmother because she was afraid. That was going to remain a sore spot in the memory, and nothing that Frank could say or do was ever going to rub it completely away.

Should she mention it now? No, let Cathy take the lead, decided Paula. Except that there was one thing she really must ask. The sight of the new receptionist had reminded her.

"Cathy," she said, "have you heard anything of Carlos? I hope he's not still waiting by the roadside for somebody to rescue him and his car."

"Oh, didn't I tell you?" Cathy had taken a large bite of walnut cake and was speaking with her mouth full. She swallowed and went on, "Carlos is fine. He called last night and said he'd got the car fixed and he had decided to take off for a few days' holiday. He's getting tired of the Gainsboroughs picking on him and he's found himself another job for when he gets back that he can combine with his studies."

"You mean he came to see you in Oxford?" said Paula, feeling relieved, yet somehow disbelieving.

"Oh no." Cathy looked surprised. Then her face cleared. "I guess it's that Anglo-American confusion again. I mean he called up on the telephone."

"Where from?"

"I don't know. Somewhere in Oxfordshire, I guess. Dad didn't say. I don't think he was quite sure himself. It was a pay phone, and the money was running out."

"Did you speak to him?" asked Paula.

"No." Again a slight clouding of the brightness. "I was in the kitchen fixing us a meal when he called."

Paula wanted to ask whether Cathy had actually heard the tele-

phone ring, but decided that this would reveal too much of her own
scepticism. Fortunately Cathy did not need any prompting, but was
eager to explain further.

"I thought it might be you calling," she said, "so I came out of the
kitchen to be ready to speak to you, and I heard Dad speaking, but
didn't know who was on the line. Then I heard him say, 'Okay,
Carlos, thanks for telling me. I'll let Cathy know. Best of luck.'
Something like that he was saying—the living-room door was open
and I could hear clearly, and I ran in and said, 'Hi, Dad, I'd like to
speak to Carlos,' but he had rung off. I must say I was rather disappointed because I'd been thinking about Carlos and wondering how
and where he was. But if his money had run out and he hadn't got
another coin . . ."

Cathy's voice trailed away.

"Do you think," said Paula carefully, feeling it might be safe to
venture on this question, "that your father perhaps didn't want you
to speak to him?"

"That's just what I did think," said Cathy, disposing of another
mouthful of cake. "Maybe he's just a little bit jealous. Or maybe—
you see, Dad is very English now and I suppose I'm really more
American. I mean, I don't get this English social-class thing. Maybe
Carlos isn't high-class enough for a close acquaintance. But I like
him. He's helped me a lot. I'm glad he's got a better job and
I'll get a chance to thank him some time or other."

Paula found this speech very interesting on two counts. First, because it revealed Cathy for the first time being openly critical of her
father. Only very mildly critical, but quite definitely showing that
there had been a difference of opinion. There would be more differ-
ences, thought Paula, once the reality began to take over from the
dream.

But even more interesting than this changed attitude of Cathy's
were the facts that her account of this little incident revealed. The
telephone had rung, and Frank had spoken on the phone as if he
were speaking to Carlos.

Perhaps he had been; or perhaps he had only wished Cathy to
believe so. How easy for him to cut off some other caller when he
became aware that Cathy had come to the living-room door, and

pretend to be talking to Carlos. He had the best possible excuse for not handing the phone to her: The caller was on a pay phone and the money had run out. Cathy assumed the call to be genuine; she would have no means of knowing otherwise until she asked Carlos about it herself. Neither would Paula.

Nevertheless, Cathy was disturbed. She suspected that her father wanted to keep her and Carlos apart, either for reasons of social snobbery or of jealousy or of both. Paula suspected it, too, but for different reasons. Either it had not been the boy at all, but arranged so that Cathy would stop wondering about him; or else it had been Carlos, but the conversation had been very different from what Frank had said.

I am back at the theory that Frank and Carlos are somehow in league together, thought Paula as she ate her own piece of cake, and that is something I can't possibly mention to Cathy.

So all she said was, "I'm very glad to hear that he's having some time off and has found another job. He's well out of this place."

"Oh, do you think so?" Cathy looked around the shabby-elegant room. "I thought he was doing quite well here. And the Gainsboroughs aren't so bad."

Paula bit back a sharp retort. Of course, Cathy doesn't know what I know about them, she reminded herself. This conversation was becoming more and more difficult, with plenty of goodwill between them but no true understanding. Although there is no reason I shouldn't tell Cathy about the Gainsboroughs, Paula thought; they are nothing to do with her father. But immediately afterwards she decided against this. She must not start gossiping about them until she had been to the police, and the thoughts of explaining her eavesdropping became more and more distasteful as the hours went by. Suppose the inspector did not believe her story? Supposing he asked other awkward questions about Mrs. Merton and Cathy?

One could not tell only part of a story; or at any rate, not being a good liar, Paula could not do so. I will do it after the inquest, she promised herself, in the same way as she might have said to herself, "I'll do it after Christmas," or "after my holiday," or after any other landmark, in order to gain a respite from a nagging conscience.

The inquest on Mrs. Merton. Here was a subject that she and Cathy could surely talk about in safety.

"I've been meaning to ask you," she said. "I thought maybe Inspector Beal would have been in touch, but he hasn't. What is the position as regards our evidence on Thursday? Do we have to change our statements, now that it is known who Mrs. Merton was?"

"Oh, that's all right," said Cathy confidently, and appearing to be herself relieved at the change of subject. "Dad will explain everything. You and I just have to stick to our statements of how we found her. We've checked all that with the inspector. We have to say what actually happened, and not give any theories. They don't want theories from witnesses, only facts."

So Frank Merton will stage-manage the whole thing again, said Paula to herself. Why should it worry her? Was that not the best way for this business to end? A verdict of accidental death, and nobody accused of anything—except that she really must, after the inquest, tell the police about the Gainsboroughs and explain away her own delay as best she could.

"That's a relief," she said aloud. "I've been rather dreading giving evidence. I've never been involved in anything like this before."

"Nor have I, but Dad says we're not to worry. It's all very straightforward. Dr. Allen will explain about my granny taking too many tablets. You and I just say our little piece. And Dad says, Paula—and this is what I meant to ask you at once, only somehow we got sort of sidetracked—please will you come back to Oxford with us after the inquest, and stay to dinner and stay the night. Dad's a very good cook, I've discovered, and that will give us a chance really to get to know you properly, without any crisis going on."

"It's very kind of you," said Paula, desperate to find an acceptable excuse for refusing, but not being able to think of anything that didn't sound too abrupt.

"Do come," urged Cathy. "It'll be so nice to get back to normal life after all that's been going on."

To this Paula could only heartily agree. "But I think I've got a meeting that evening," she added. "I'll have to check in my diary. It's in the office."

"Can't you miss it?"

Paula felt ashamed that her feeble lie should be so readily believed. "I'll let you know tomorrow," she said. "Will that be all right?" She stood up. "Shall we go upstairs for you to collect your things? I ought to be going soon."

"You're sure you don't mind coming?"

"Not a bit."

But Paula did mind. It would take some very happy and positive experiences in Bloomsbury Lodge to efface the unpleasant impressions that she had collected there. She no longer had any desire to explore or investigate anything, simply to do the job quickly and to get away.

Cathy, too, was not anxious to linger. Almost in silence they emptied the clothes closet and the drawers of the chest, filling two suitcases.

"I've got some more in the store-room downstairs," said Cathy, "that I've not even opened yet. I'll write to Mrs. Gainsborough and say we'll collect them later, when Dad's here with the car. I don't want to talk to her now. Do you?"

"No, not now," said Paula. Part of her reluctance to be here was, in fact, due to the fear of meeting Marjorie Gainsborough, but they came out of the building without any embarrassing encounters and found a taxi for Cathy almost immediately.

On the bus going home Paula tried to think of a valid excuse for declining the invitation, but failed. When James arrived she told him about it at once and added that she wished he was invited, too.

"So do I," he said. "It would make a much more suitable dinner party. Can't you get me in?"

"I don't see how. Anyway, I'm only concerned with getting myself out of it."

"I think you ought to go."

"Why?" demanded Paula. "Why are you so keen on pushing me into an involvement with Cathy and Frank?"

"So you'd noticed that, had you? I'll tell you why, love. Because it's the only way to get them out of your system."

"Are you saying that the best way to get me to do something is to keep urging me not to do it? Am I really such a contrary sort of person?"

James laughed. "That was the idea at first, but now I honestly think that you're never going to get clear of Frank Merton if you never find out whether he's a complete baddie or just a sort of average baddie like the rest of us. Besides, I want to know as well. I'm curious."

"You are the limit, James. First you get all steamed up because I put myself into dangerous situations, and then you turn right round and start trying to shove me into them."

"Yes, I know. Why should inconsistency be a woman's privilege? In any case, since when have you regarded consistency as a virtue? Personally, I think it's just boring."

"It depends on the situation," said Paula. "You wouldn't want inconsistency in a bus driver. Or a surgeon. Anyway, let's save the subject for our candlelit dinner," she added hastily, as James seemed to be about to pursue the discussion, "and do help me. Please. I know I'm going to end up going to Oxford, and I'm scared. Really scared."

"Would you like to go over the whole business, since you and Cathy made your gruesome discovery, and try to find out just what likelihood there is that Frank Merton believes you to be a threat to him?"

"Would you mind? Wouldn't it bore you?"

"Come on. Set our academic minds to work, sorting out firm facts from theoretical possibilities."

They did this over their dinner, a salmon pie which Paula had made because he liked it, followed by a great deal of vanilla ice cream with hot chocolate sauce, which was a favourite with them both. Their conclusions, although helped along by strong coffee and Benedictine, were not very inspiring.

"We haven't got a single shred of proof that Frank has murdered anybody," said James. "Just a host of possibilities."

"Do you think he has?"

"I think these two deaths have occurred very conveniently for him. Now. What have you said or done—I mean said or done as opposed to thinking and suspecting—that might make Frank realise you suspect him?"

"I can't think of anything specific," said Paula slowly, "except that if it was Frank who was behind the curtains in the attic flat next door to Bloomsbury Lodge, and if he saw me climbing about on the roof . . ."

"But you didn't see him. Could he possibly think that you might have seen him?"

"No, but I spoke to the caretaker next door. I wish I hadn't."

"So do I. Yes, this is rather awkward." James thought for a while. "It's all very vague," he said at last. "If the subject of the Bloomsbury Lodge roof should crop up, you can be perfectly honest and say you didn't want to be caught up there in one of the attic rooms."

"But why was I up there in the first place?"

"Snooping. You'll have to admit you were snooping. Let him think you suspect Joe Gainsborough. Tell him about the thefts, if you're really pressed."

"And what about my snooping in Dr. Frend's house?"

"If he gets to know of that, you'll have to admit that you did have your suspicions of him, but not of killing anybody, only of pretending to be Cathy's father when he wasn't. And that's perfectly true as well. You did have your suspicions."

"So you think the purpose of this invitation is to find out what I know?"

"One of the purposes," replied James. "The other one is to modify or elaborate on his own story. Your best plan will be to follow his lead. He's vain enough to think he can get away with anything."

"He's very vain," agreed Paula.

"And I don't think he's going to murder you just because he suspects you of not trusting him. After all, these two deaths were easily contrived. A feeble old woman and a sick old man. You come into quite a different category. The best line to take, if I may presume to offer advice on such a matter, is to pretend you've fallen for him."

"Darling James, you are such a comfort. I do wish you could come to Oxford with me."

"Maybe we can fix some checking-up times."

"Will you come to the inquest?"

"Of course. And now may we please go and watch 'Dallas.' I feel I need distraction."

"You shall have it. And for once I will join you. Who said I was too rigidly academic and would never relax?"

CHAPTER 12

Paula had indeed been apprehensive about the inquest. She sat with Frank and Cathy and the other witnesses near the front of the courtroom and was very glad, just before the first case was called, to see James come in and sit near the back. She had never been to an inquest before and was both surprised and relieved to see the calm and reassuring manner in which it was conducted.

They listened to the story of the suicide of a teenage boy, and while giving evidence the father broke down and wept uncontrollably. He was led away and allowed to recover in peace while the boy's aunt took over the story. The coroner consulted with his colleagues —all of them nondescript, greying men in dark suits—and stated the verdict with what seemed to be sincere human sympathy and regret.

Paula turned round as the unhappy little family group left the court, caught James's eye, and knew he was feeling much the same as she was herself. The impact of such a tragedy momentarily dwarfed all her own preoccupations, and the bare factual account was more moving than any number of sensational newspaper reports.

"Poor things," said Frank lightly. "But they were very dim not to see that the boy was taking drugs. Cheer up, Cathy. It's nothing to do with us."

Cathy looked shocked and upset. Paula thought it wisest to say nothing, and was glad when the case of Mrs. Eileen Mary Merton was called.

Inspector Beal said his piece, and then it was Paula's turn. It was so simple, just repeating in this unthreatening atmosphere exactly what had happened, that she could not understand why she had built up such a mental blockage about it.

A short consultation followed her statement, and it was decided that there was no need to call Cathy to give evidence. Dr. Allen then expounded, in considerable detail, on the state of Mrs. Merton's heart and circulation and the medication she had been taking. Joe Gainsborough said that from the little he had seen of Mrs. Merton, she had never struck him as in danger of taking her own life, and everything seemed to be rumbling on very much as planned until Frank took the stand and produced, for Paula at any rate, a startling revelation in almost his very first words.

"Your name is Frank Henry Merton?"

"Yes."

"And you are the son of the deceased?"

"Not the son," corrected Frank. "Mrs. Merton was my father's second wife. My mother died thirty years ago."

So that was the solution. Paula had no doubt that Frank was capable of telling lies on oath, but this statement had the ring of truth. It fitted all round. The genuine Frank Merton, Cathy's father, hence the strong resemblance between them. But not the son of the dead woman. One of Paula's chief, but only half-conscious reasons for believing that Frank was not the genuine article was her reluctance to think that he could have killed his mother.

With this information the whole impersonation theory finally collapsed like a house of cards, but Paula's suspicions that he was a murderer became stronger than ever. She glanced at Cathy to see whether this was a revelation to the girl as well, but Cathy was staring at her father with such a loving and admiring look that it was plain that she had received no sudden shock.

Of course he had told her, thought Paula, that Mrs. Merton was no blood relation of hers. That would have comforted Cathy a lot. It was worrying her so much, that she had missed the chance of getting to know her own grandmother. But he definitely gave the impression, Paula's thoughts ran on, when we first met him, that Mrs. Merton was his real mother. Why?

The answer came only too easily. The meeting with Frank at Dr. Frend's house had been very brief and very much dominated by the death of Dr. Frend. It was not the moment for explaining in detail the family relationships.

Paula took a grip on her thoughts and listened to what Frank was saying.

The state of mind of his stepmother, Mrs. Eileen Merton. Yes, she had always been of a nervous disposition, an excellent housekeeper, a perfectionist. The responsibility of looking after Dr. Frend was beginning to worry her a great deal. She badly needed a break, and she had come to London for a few days rather than go to a quiet country hotel. Naturally she came to Bloomsbury Lodge, because of their own connections with the place.

Yes, there had been another occasion recently when she had become confused after taking her pills. Very confused. When she recovered, she admitted that she had forgotten she had taken any and had swallowed some more.

The questioning went on, moving slowly and inexorably towards a verdict of accidental death. Frank spoke quietly, but without any hesitation. Paula had the impression that he was deliberately presenting himself in muted colours. The whole personality seemed to be subdued; even the eyes looked less vividly blue. There was not the slightest sign, either in Frank or in any of the other witnesses, of an explosion of painful human emotion such as had characterised the previous case.

The coroner conferred with his colleagues and made his pronouncement. While Frank was conferring with one of the court officials, Paula took the opportunity to talk to James.

"Don't forget what we've arranged," she murmured.

"I haven't forgotten. This evening I shall be staying at home drafting exam questions. During the course of the evening I shall have to consult you urgently by telephone. Maybe more than once. I've got the Oxford phone number."

"Thanks, love."

Paula turned to Cathy, who had come up to join them. "Not so bad, was it?"

"So she wasn't your grandmother after all," said James. "That came as a surprise to me, but I guess it was a relief to you."

"That's right. You know"—she turned to Paula—"how bad I felt about not having talked to her. I still feel bad, but not as much as if she had been."

"Did you know, Paula?" asked James.

"No, I didn't know."

"I wanted to tell you, but Dad said not to." Cathy looked apologetically at Paula.

At that moment Frank joined the group. "She didn't like it to be known," he said. "Prescott never knew either. The world must be full of this sort of innocent concealment, that only comes to light for the purposes of official records."

"All those respectably married people who turn out to have been living in sin," said James. "Did you find somewhere to park?"

They moved out of the building, James and Frank walking ahead and discussing the difficulty of car parking in London, and Paula and Cathy some way behind them, talking about Mrs. Merton.

"In a way," said Cathy, "it's rather a relief that she's gone. That sounds awful, but Dad says she was going to be quite a responsibility for him as she got more and more forgetful. He'd been wondering whether he ought to get in somebody else to look after Dr. Frend, but of course she didn't want to give way to another woman in the house. It was bad enough with the nurses. He says his stepmother was always complaining about them and they about her."

A very familiar story, thought Paula. If this was going to be the main topic of conversation for the evening, then it was going to be tedious but hardly alarming. Maybe this was the reason for the invitation: to immerse her in the problems of a household of feeble elderly people, and thus flush away the last shreds of suspicion from her mind.

"We now think," continued Cathy as they neared the car park, "that it must have been Mrs. Merton, and not one of the nurses, who let Dr. Frend have the whisky."

"That sounds very possible," said Paula, wondering whether Cathy was consciously carrying out her father's instructions, but forbearing to add that Mrs. Merton had not been near Dr. Frend for several days before his death, and that surely the fatal combination of drugs and alcohol would not have taken so long to have its effect. But if that was to be the story, then no doubt Frank would have a good explanation for everything.

Was it all going to be explained through Cathy? Or would he at some point take over himself? Half of Paula was still very nervous and apprehensive and reluctant to face the evening ahead; but the other half, the intellectually inquisitive half, was fascinated by the prospect of observing the mind that had planned this visit of hers.

"Apparently the old man was very fond of his whisky and was crying for it like a baby when his mind got confused," said Cathy. "Dad says his stepmother liked it, too, although she wasn't supposed to be taking any alcohol either, with her heart condition. Did you know that there is a sort of secret cupboard in one of the columns of that four-poster bed?"

"Good Lord, is there really?"

Paula was intrigued and could not help showing it. Cathy was obviously pleased at the effect of her words, but had no opportunity to say anything more at that moment, since they had now arrived at Frank's car, a similar model to James's, but silver-grey instead of white.

Apprehension triumphed over curiosity as they drove away, and was aggravated by the discovery that Frank was an erratic driver, even worse than James. Cathy, sitting in the back, appeared not to notice their jerky and sometimes dangerous progress.

But after a while she said, "We aren't in any hurry, Dad. Can't we go the scenic route? It's so pretty with all the little boats on the river, and that nice old bridge."

"She means Henley Regatta course," explained Frank to Paula. "Okay by you?"

Paula said she would be delighted, which was true. First of all, they would have to go more slowly than on the motorway, and second, since they would be going through the area where Frank said Carlos's car had broken down, there might even be an opportunity to mention this without arousing suspicion and maybe even to learn something.

When it came to the point, however, Frank was talking in detail about the condition of Bloomsbury Lodge under the wardenship of Arnold Frend twenty years ago, and she could not possibly interrupt.

It was interesting, and also gratifying, to find that she and James had guessed more or less correctly what had happened at that time.

"I knew of Dr. Frend from having gone to some of his lectures when I was at college," said Frank. "He didn't remember me, of course, from among hundreds of students. The place was in almost as bad a condition as it is now. The woman who looked after the bookings had just walked out and the accounts were in an indescribable muddle."

He laughed, took a sharp corner much too fast, missed an oncoming vehicle by inches, and laughed again.

Cathy gave a little squeal. "These English lanes!" she exclaimed. "Why didn't they build them straight?"

"They were respecting the sacredness of property," said Frank. "Nothing must cut through my land. The road will just have to wander round the outside of it."

"Then don't let's go so fast," said Cathy quite sharply. "I want to see the little boats on the river."

Paula felt grateful to Cathy for temporary relief from her more immediate fears, and wondered whether the girl really was gaining some influence over her father after all. It might simply be, however, that he was going carefully with her until he was sure of her money.

During the course of the evening it became plain that Cathy was capable of standing up for herself and was by no means uncritical of him. The joy of their reunion had certainly not worn off and probably never would, coloured as it was by Cathy's cherished dim memory of her father and by the years of longing and dreaming. But the dream would have to come to terms with Cathy's adult mind and adult observation, and Paula could envisage a situation where a somewhat disillusioned Cathy treated her father with a sort of affectionate indulgence, loving him in spite of his faults.

This was, of course, assuming that those faults were no worse than the average. Would Cathy's loyalty hold if it were ever to be discovered that he had actually killed for gain?

"I wanted us to eat in the dining-room with all the best china and silver and glass," said Cathy as they came into the house in Clarendon Place, "but Dad said it wouldn't be suitable. So I hope you don't mind us eating in the kitchen, as we usually do."

Paula was relieved to hear this. She still had very much the sensation of intruding into somebody else's home, even though the mortal remains of Dr. Arnold Frend were now in a chapel of rest, awaiting burial, and Frank Merton was the lawful inheritor of the property.

The watercress soup, which Frank had made, was as excellent as

Cathy had promised, and for a little while they talked of nothing but food.

"I want Dad to turn this house into a hotel," said Cathy. "Very exclusive and very expensive. There's a shortage of good hotels round here."

Paula, wondering how serious this suggestion was meant to be, made a non-committal reply. Frank merely laughed.

"She's afraid I'm not going to have enough to occupy myself," he said. "Cathy has the usual American horror of inactivity. Do you think I am lazy, Paula?"

"I've no means of judging," said Paula as casually as she could. "I don't know you well enough."

"No more than I know you. But at least you now believe that I really am Frank Merton. You didn't at first, did you?"

"I thought Cathy would be wiser not to take anything for granted," said Paula cautiously. "All I knew was that she had come to England to try to find her father, who was last heard of in London twenty years ago and hadn't been heard from since. She didn't know then—and I certainly didn't know then—that Bill Prescott was masterminding the whole thing."

"And you thought Cathy could be taken in by some impostor scenting some advantage?"

"I never would!" cried Cathy indignantly, sparing Paula the effort of replying. "I wasn't born yesterday."

"If you still have any lingering suspicions of me," said Frank, ignoring the interruption and continuing to look closely at Paula, "you're very welcome to see Prescott's letter. Cathy has read it. I've got it upstairs."

There was a noticeable hesitation before Paula replied, with an embarrassment that she was quite unable to conceal, "Of course I don't want to see it. It's none of my business. Except that," she went on more confidently, "I couldn't help wondering whether you'd been in touch with him and told him that you two had got together. It's not really my business either, but he did telephone me after Cathy left Bloomsbury Lodge and asked me if I knew where she was. I didn't know then, of course, but I said I'd let him know when I found her. Which I haven't done. I assume you've been in touch?"

"Cathy called him last Sunday," said Frank. "I didn't want to speak to him. Dead friendships are best not disinterred."

"Dead friendships," repeated Paula thoughtfully. It struck her as rather a strange expression. "No, I suppose not," she added.

"You ought to have spoken to him, Dad," said Cathy. "I know he felt hurt."

Frank made no comment.

"I'd so hoped you would become friends again," persisted Cathy, "you and Uncle Bill. It would—sort of—make it all complete."

"You can't reconstruct the past, child," said Frank. "In any case, you're leaving out the most important character of all. What about your mother? Do you want to bring us together as well?"

It was not said particularly unkindly, but without any warning Cathy burst into tears, tried to control herself, failed, and jumped up and ran out of the room.

"Excuse me," said Frank, and got up and followed her.

Paula helped herself to cheese. It seemed a bit heartless to go on placidly eating, but the Stilton looked very good, and it was a relief to be alone for a little while, and there was really nothing she could do for Cathy at this moment. The dream had come true; but like all dreams, it was not under the dreamer's control. The detached observer part of Paula waited to see how the clash of wills was going to resolve itself.

Frank was gone for several minutes. "Sorry about that," he said when he returned. "She'll be down later. Shall we have our coffee in the sitting-room?"

A wood fire, burning brightly, and a red-shaded standard lamp made a little area of warmth and comfort in the vast room.

"Do you think I ought to give in to Cathy over Prescott?" asked Frank, sounding as if he genuinely wanted to hear Paula's opinion.

"I can't possibly tell," she replied. "As I said, I hardly know anything about any of you."

"Of course you don't. I'd better tell you."

Paula prepared herself to hear Frank's version of the story, and as it proceeded she began to wonder whether Cathy's fit of hysterics had been deliberately provoked, to provide an opportunity for this tête-à-tête.

"Her mother is also Cathy," said Frank. "Sounds like *Wuthering Heights,* doesn't it?—but don't cast me in the role of Heathcliff. This is a very different sort of story. If you have been imagining some kind of 1960s flower-people's commune, then you're dead right. That's how it was. Make love, not war. There was certainly no grand passion involved. I am quite incapable of any such thing, and Cathy's mother always was a hardheaded little bitch. Slumming it among the hippies in order to torment her relations, but very well aware of the million-dollar safety net to fall back into whenever she got bored with the squalor."

"And were you aware of it, too?" asked Paula. "Was that the intention at the time?"

He laughed without the least trace of embarrassment. "Ah, you've got my measure. Wealth. Comfort. Yes, that's my passion. My guiding star."

"So you would do anything for money?" said Paula, trying to sound equally light-hearted.

"Not quite anything. I have my limits. I've been lucky, so far, not to be driven to them."

Paula poured herself some more coffee. The warmth and the sparking logs and the sense of being shut away from the wind and wet of the outside world were having a hypnotic effect on her. Keep it cool, she told herself; keep it casual. There was no use pretending she had no suspicions of him. The best she could do was convince him that she had no firm grounds for any suspicions.

This was the truth. She had no firm evidence at all. It should not be difficult for her to hold on to the truth.

"Prescott thought Cathy's mother and I were in love," went on Frank. "He really believed in the love-not-war thing. Rich girl loves poor boy. Child on the way. Welcome home to the Bradshaw millions and happiness ever after. That was his rosy dream. An incurable romantic, as I said. And Cathy—my Cathy—seems to have imbibed something of it from him over the years. But there's also a generous measure of her mother's hardheadedness, I'm glad to say."

Paula made no comment. She was feeling very wide awake now and was listening with great interest.

"It didn't work out that way," went on Frank. "The Bradshaws liked their romance at a distance. Or on the screen or in a book. They would accept the child, but they wouldn't accept me. They might have done so if she'd pushed it—Cathy's mum, I mean. But she didn't push it. Would you like to guess why?"

"You'd proved unfaithful," said Paula. "Another woman? Women?"

"The plural, yes. I was getting bored with waiting for the reconciliation scene with the Bradshaw parents. Their daughter didn't know about it at first, but Prescott found out and began to lecture me. Not for being a fool to risk my inheritance, but for letting Cathy down. We are poles apart, you see, Prescott and myself. I valued him once —as a sort of foil, I suppose. He valued me. Can't think why."

Paula could guess. It was a not uncommon basis for friendship. The dimmer of the two gaining a sort of reflected glory from the bright one. But there was bound to be resentment and envy in this sort of unequal partnership.

Frank's next words bore this out.

"I tell you why I don't want to have anything more to do with Prescott," he said, offering Paula a cigarette and taking one himself. "He told Cathy about my other women. Okay, so I am a bastard and always have been and always will be, and I'd no intention of being faithful to her and of course she did much better for herself than if she'd married me, and if she had married me, we'd probably have been divorced within a year or two. I'm not making any pretences; I've got no morals at all. But what he did to me, I wouldn't have done to anybody. Sneak stuff. I can't forget it. I can't forgive it. That really did go beyond the limit."

He threw his unfinished cigarette into the fire and instantly lit another.

Paula watched him, fascinated. She had not believed it possible that he would ever reveal any strong genuine emotion about anything, but he was certainly doing so now. This long-ago betrayal still rankled. So that was his sticking-point, his limit beyond which he would not go. Murder—and she was more and more convinced that he was a murderer—was acceptable; telling tales behind a friend's back was not.

"I suppose," she said after they had sat in silence for a moment or two, "that Cathy—young Cathy—knows nothing of this?"

"She knows nothing. That much I do have to thank Prescott for. He must have felt guilty about it, because apparently he's been encouraging her to build up an idealised picture of me over all these years. God knows how I'm going to live up to it, but I'm going to try, for a while at least, because I'm determined to have some share in the Bradshaw millions. It's certainly due to me. I'd have had it years ago if it hadn't been for Prescott."

"At least you make no secret of your motives," said Paula.

"Why should I? I am entirely mercenary. But it also happens that I've rather taken to Cathy. You'll find this hard to believe, but I was actually quite fond of the child."

"I don't find it hard to believe," said Paula. "She has good memories of you. Bill Prescott didn't invent those for her. They are her own, and genuine."

Frank stared into the fire, saying nothing. It was impossible to guess what was in his mind. They seemed to have come to a complete stop, and Paula was glad when the telephone rang.

Frank answered it. "Paula? Yes, she's right here. I'll go and fetch Cathy," he said to Paula, handing her the instrument, "while you're talking."

James was very apologetic about disturbing her, but there was this essay question for the finals paper on twentieth-century literature that had got to be settled by tomorrow, so he thought . . .

Paula answered his query, trying hard to convey, by tone of voice alone, that she was all right and all was going well. To say anything more was too risky; there were telephone extensions all over the house. James thanked her, apologised again, and rang off, saying, "See you tomorrow."

Paula knew that he was not reassured. He had sensed her own tension.

Was she in any danger? Was this narration of Frank's, which really amounted to a sort of confession, simply the prelude, as so often in fiction, to the disposing of the person who had provoked it?

It was best not to speculate, but to continue to watch and listen and be very wary.

"Friend James must be missing you," said Frank, coming back into the room. "Didn't want you to come?"

"That's right," said Paula. "He's checking up on me."

"I've read some of the Goff novels," said Frank, "but he's not my favourite author. Too much detailed psychological analysis. I prefer the characters to reveal themselves. James is the grandson, isn't he?"

"That's right," said Paula again.

From this it was a natural transition to Cathy's English literature studies, and the subject lasted them until Cathy herself returned.

CHAPTER 13

"Now I'm going to leave Cathy to entertain you for a little while," said Frank, "because I've got some phone calls to make, but I'll do them upstairs."

"Dad's room is two floors up," explained Cathy when he had gone. "It's almost as big as this one. He's got all his books up there and doesn't like to be disturbed. Otherwise I'd show you. But we can look at the rest of the house if you like. You are sleeping in the little room next to Dr. Frend's, and I've moved up to the floor above, next to Dad. Will that be all right? You won't be nervous?"

"Why should I be nervous?"

Paula asked the question almost as a challenge, looking closely at Cathy as they stood together in the front hall.

"To be sleeping in the room next to where someone has died," replied Cathy without any hesitation. "I guess some people wouldn't like it."

"And I guess most of us have to put up with it most of the time," retorted Paula. "People are dying all the time. Everywhere. Most people have very little choice of where they sleep. No, of course I don't mind," she added more gently, since Cathy showed signs of becoming upset again. "I hope I haven't turned you out of your room."

Cathy was pushing open a door opposite the main living-room, and she did not reply.

"This is Dr. Frend's library," she said. "It's never used. I don't know what Dad is going to do about it."

Paula could never resist books.

"It would be a pity to break it up," she said after a quick look round. "If I were a historian I would grab at the lot. There are some rare items here, I believe."

"They are all catalogued," said Cathy, coming to join her in the far corner near the bay window. "Dad knows exactly what is in this house. He pretends to be very lazy, but he isn't. Not really. He can't stick to any profession, but he's got a teacher's diploma and he did his law exams when he was helping Dr. Frend. I never know what I'm going to find out about him next. That's very English, isn't it, to keep quiet about your achievements."

"I suppose so," murmured Paula, still looking at the books, but nevertheless listening intently to what Cathy was saying.

"I shouldn't be surprised to find he had other qualifications as well. He's good at drawing, too. My dad is very gifted, Paula, and maybe that's the difficulty. If you're good at a lot of things you don't stay with any one of them. But I still think he ought to follow a profession or manage a business, don't you? He could have a law office where the clerks do most of the work, but it would sound so much better if I could say my dad's a lawyer. I hate to think people look down on him because he's spent his time taking care of an old man. What do you think, Paula?"

"I can't believe for a moment that anybody looks down on your father," said Paula, straightening up.

"But they do," cried Cathy. "Oxford is a terribly snobby place, I find. If we are going to stay here, then I want him to be respected."

This sounded to Paula rather like a volte-face, the sort of inconsistency that James seemed to approve of. Only a few days ago Cathy had been complaining of her father's snobbish attitude towards Carlos; now she seemed to have taken it over herself.

"Then maybe it's not such a good idea to suggest that your father should run a hotel," said Paula.

"Oh yes. That would be fine. I've been researching present-day English attitudes towards social status these last two days," went on Cathy, quite seriously. "I don't mean any academic or statistical research, but I guess my conclusions have some validity. I've been talking to people and reading magazine ads and articles. It's socially acceptable to manage an exclusive hotel. A small stately home, or somewhere with historical interest. You have to do your own cooking, of course, and be very snobby about food and wine. And your guests are hand-picked."

Paula could not help laughing. "Your poor father. He'll begin to regret that you found him."

"I found him just in time," said Cathy. "He does have a tiny tendency to be lazy, in spite of what I just said and in spite of all the things he can do. While Dr. Frend and Mrs. Merton were alive he had some sort of excuse, because they really could not manage here without his help, but they are both dead now, and if it weren't for me, Dad would just stay on here getting old and fat and lazy."

"I'm sure he wouldn't," protested Paula, but to herself she was saying, If you weren't here, Cathy, it's more than likely that neither of the old people would yet be dead.

"Have you seen enough of the library?" asked Cathy. "Shall we go upstairs now?"

Paula reminded herself that she must pretend to have seen nothing on the next floor except the bathroom.

"Here's your bedroom," said Cathy, pushing open a door. "I ought to have shown you before. Dad brought your things up. I hope you'll be comfortable and not too cold."

"It's beautifully warm," said Paula. "I see your desire to be English does not extend to a toleration of cold houses."

Cathy smiled. "It's not my doing. It's Dad. He likes to be comfortable. For myself I don't care. You know that, Paula. I was quite contented in Bloomsbury Lodge. Shall we go on now? I want to show you something, but we'll save it until last."

The rest of the house was much as Paula had expected. Cathy opened doors to rooms, cupboards, and attics, some smelling rather musty, but none revealing anything in the least bit mysterious or suspicious.

"We can't go into Dad's room," she concluded, "but now we'll go to Dr. Frend's. If you don't mind going where someone has died," she added.

"Are we to view the body?" asked Paula lightly.

Cathy looked rather shocked. "He's in a chapel of rest. The funeral is next Monday."

"And Mrs. Merton's funeral?"

"That will be the day after. At Wilsham. Dad says she wanted to be buried in her home village. He spoke to the vicar there—you remember, the one I saw when I was trying to trace the family when I first got to England. He was very pleased to hear that we had found each other."

"And will you be going to these funerals?"

"Of course. I can't let Dad go on his own. And now," went on Cathy, leading the way into Dr. Frend's bedroom, "I'm going to show you how Dr. Frend died."

Paula said nothing. If Frank had been present, he would have guessed at once that this was not the first time she had been in the room, but Cathy was less perceptive.

"We thought you would be interested, Dad and I," continued Cathy, "because you were actually in the house when it happened."

"Last Saturday afternoon," murmured Paula, thinking that it would look odd if she continued to make no comment, but feeling quite sure that whatever she was going to be told would not be the truth.

"It's here, at this corner." Cathy was standing by the bed, on the very spot where Paula had picked up the copy of *The Times*. "This is the bedpost with the hidden cupboard."

"Of course. You mentioned it this afternoon." Paula came closer. "I've heard about such things, but never seen one."

"It opens with a spring," said Cathy. "Look. It's very easy to work. You don't have to use much force."

A section of the carved oak swung open, revealing a space large enough to contain a bottle twice the size of the one that had been found on the bedside table.

"Dad never knew about this cache," said Cathy. "Nor did Dr. Allen or any of the nurses. But Dad is sure that Mrs. Merton knew. She'd looked after the cleaning of the house for years. She must have come across it when she polished the furniture."

"That sounds quite likely," said Paula, feeling that further comment was called for.

"So I guess she was responsible, really, for him dying like that," said Cathy, "although she wasn't actually here. She must have bought the whisky for him, because it's certain that nobody else did, and left it where the old man could easily get hold of it. It must have been going on for months. It could have killed him at any time."

It could have, if that is indeed what happened, thought Paula, but in fact it did not kill him until the very convenient moment when Mrs. Merton, herself dead, could take all the blame, and when Dr. Frend himself was beginning to be rather in the way.

Perhaps there had been a fear that the old man might alter his will, a classic motive for murder.

"I wonder whether the doctor or the nurses ever suspected," Paula said aloud.

"I don't know about the nurses. They don't come regularly. Only at nights or when Mrs. Merton was away. But Dr. Allen says that he did have his suspicions, and he mentioned them to Mrs. Merton. Of course she denied it." Cathy shut the little door, which instantly blended with the rest of the carved oak of the bedpost. "She's dead now," she went on, "so there's no need for anybody else to know about this, and Dad thinks it best if we all try to forget it, but he knew you would be interested and he wanted you to know."

She paused, and then added in quite a different tone of voice, "He likes you, Paula. D'you fancy being a stepmother?"

Paula laughed. "Not in the least. Nor a wife either. Never again. I think your father is lovely, Cathy, but he certainly would not look at me, and I wouldn't trust him an inch."

"I didn't think so. I don't blame you."

They moved towards the door of the room, Cathy purposefully as if pleased with the successful carrying out of a task, but Paula more slowly, wondering how she was going to get back to the subject of Dr. Frend's death after this unexpected diversion.

At the door she paused and looked back into the room.

"It's very sad," she said, "to end like that after what was really a very distinguished career. For a scholar to lose his mental faculties— that's dreadful. I suppose he must have been completely confused. Unless he was quite clear in mind and deliberately took the whisky with the drugs, hoping to end it all. What do you think, Cathy?"

"Dad thought of that, too, but he says we shall never know. Dr. Frend had lucid moments sometimes, but most of the time he was either asleep or muddled."

Cathy made a movement to open the door; this continued discussion was plainly not part of her brief. Paula knew that she ought to accept the account of Dr. Frend's death without question and without showing undue interest, but her fatal curiosity was taking over again, and she went on, knowing it to be unwise.

"But what did you think yourself, Cathy? After all, he was still alive last Friday night when you were here, and didn't die until late Saturday afternoon, when you were entertaining James and myself. Did you think he might have deliberately taken the whisky? I know you were terribly upset."

"I guess I was just overwrought. Finding Mrs. Merton dead and then finding Dad—it was all a bit overwhelming."

Paula murmured something sympathetic, mentally kicking herself for having made such a bungle of this conversation. She ought never to have reverted to the subject of Dr. Frend's death. All that had come of it was that she had aroused Cathy's suspicions and had learned nothing at all. The conversation would be repeated to Frank at the earliest possible moment and he would instantly know that Paula was still nosing around.

That *Times,* for instance. Paula had noticed today's edition lying on a coffee-table in the sitting-room. Had Dr. Frend had a separate copy for himself? If so, its absence must surely be noticed. Even more would it be noticed if the only copy in the house was missing. Frank would know that the old man was in the habit of doing the crossword puzzle; Frank would wonder where the paper was, would ask the doctor, ask the nurse, would ask Cathy herself, would work out by process of elimination who there was in the house who could have taken it away. . . .

"I'd like to use the bathroom now, if that's all right," she said to Cathy as the latter was suggesting that they should go down to the sitting-room. It had become absolutely imperative to have a few moments of privacy to take stock of the present situation.

Safe in the bathroom, Paula thought over the events of the evening so far. There had been some revelations about the past from Frank, which she was inclined to believe, because they made sense. But the explaining of recent events had been left to Cathy.

Why? Presumably because it sounded more convincing. Or was it because he knew she would be more at ease with Cathy, and therefore more likely to give herself away?

In general, however, the evening up till now had not been particularly nerve-wracking. The worst moment had been her own fault—her persistent questions about Dr. Frend's death. Even if Cathy did not mention this to her father, it was very worrying to Paula to find she could be so indiscreet, and it did not augur well for any direct confrontation with Frank.

Was this to take place, or had the purpose of her visit been accomplished?

James had suggested that there were two main purposes: One was to elaborate on the story, and this had certainly taken place. But the other purpose—to find out how much Paula actually knew, or even how much she suspected—had scarcely been touched on. It wasn't very late; there was plenty of time for more talk.

But there was not much more time for remaining in the bathroom. A few more minutes might justifiably be spent in the bedroom, unpacking her night things.

But I can't possibly stay the night in this house.

The thought came with such force into Paula's mind that she believed she had spoken it aloud. For a few panicky moments she had no purpose save immediate escape.

She actually opened the bathroom window—it was an old-fashioned sash-window, with frosted glass—and peered outside. Immediately underneath, dimly visible in the light coming from the bathroom behind her, was a lilac bush, old and quite tough-looking; but the upper branches, onto which she would need to climb, were certainly not strong enough to bear her weight. Besides, she was not dressed for that sort of thing, but was wearing a dark blue and white costume suitable for attending inquests and going visiting on cool autumn evenings.

Yet the impulse to run away at once was overwhelming. If only she had arranged to have an urgent summons to her sister instead of James's useless phone call. But Stella would never have agreed to a fake. She didn't approve of Paula running around trying to solve mysteries, and would be deeply worried and unhappy if she knew of Paula's present predicament.

As no doubt James was now. Was it possible to phone him? Of course not. Not from the house, and if she were to leave the house, then she might as well run away completely, because she would never be able to bring herself to come back.

Paula shut the bathroom window.

Get out of the house. Don't think any farther ahead.

Whatever legitimate excuse could she make for leaving the house for a little while? If only she had her car here . . . How about saying she had left something she needed in Frank's car? Useless. He would offer to go and fetch it for her, or to accompany her there. She wanted to see the garden . . . in the dark? She wanted some fresh air . . . on a wet, murky evening like this? She wanted to call on an acquaintance in Oxford. . . . She had a sentimental yearning to see Magdalen Tower floodlit. . . .

Oh, stop wasting time on these idiotic excuses, she scolded herself, and get on with it. *Do* something.

She opened the bathroom door and came out onto the landing. There was no sign of Cathy. Paula ran into the little bedroom allotted to her, picked up her purse, looked longingly for a moment at her raincoat but decided it would have to stay there since it would need too much explaining if she met anybody, and came to the head of the main staircase, where she stood listening.

Where were they now? Up or down? Cathy must surely be telling Frank everything that Paula had said in Dr. Frend's room. How much did Cathy herself know, or guess?

Don't think of that now. Just keep going.

Down the main staircase, making no sound. No sound in the house at all, all closed doors and thick carpets. Luxurious and grim. An old man dying here. Helpless. How was he forced to take the fatal drink? A glass of orange juice by the bed; he would drink from it, unsuspecting, when he was sleepy and thirsty.

Don't speculate. Just get away.

The front hall. Nobody here. But voices somewhere. Very low. Behind the sitting-room door. Waiting for her. Not a second to lose. Not the front door. That would make too much noise. And she could be seen from the sitting-room window as she ran towards the gate.

The kitchen and the scullery beyond. There must be a back door. Locked? No, only bolted. The bolts moved easily and silently. None of the Bloomsbury Lodge makeshift stuff here.

The cold, wet autumn night felt to Paula like the air of freedom, wonderful to breathe, but there was no time to be wasted. No sense running down to the far end of the garden; there would be high walls all round. The tradesmen's entrance would be best, half hidden by bushes and out of sight of the main windows.

Paula was only a few feet away from the little side gate and was already rejoicing in her success when she felt herself grabbed by the arm and pulled into the shelter of the bushes.

She was too stunned for the moment even to cry out, but nevertheless a hand came up to cover her mouth and a low voice said, "Don't scream. Come along quietly."

CHAPTER 14

After the rather unsatisfactory telephone call to Paula, which took place at about half-past eight, James felt too restless to settle down to anything. He was very tempted to drive to Oxford straight away, since that would ease his need for action, but when he got there, what should he do? Sit in the car outside the house in Clarendon Place all night?

Reluctantly he rejected the idea. Not all his ingenuity could think up a halfway tolerable excuse for getting into that house.

How about the London end? One needed no excuse for walking into Bloomsbury Lodge. Mrs. Merton's death was officially recorded as accidental, but that didn't mean there was no possibility of fresh facts, of fresh gossip, coming to light.

My hypothesis, decided James as he joined the stream of cars inching their way down towards Baker Street and Central London, which I now propose to test, is as follows: Mrs. Merton was killed by the placing of a pillow over her head, probably when she was sleepy from drugs, and then put into the bath to make doubly sure and to confuse the people who found her. The perpetrator was Frank Merton, who gained access to her room by climbing along the roof parapet from the next-door attic apartment.

Perhaps it would be best to go first to the house next door. Bloomsbury Lodge would have somebody on duty all night, but the caretaker of the apartments would probably not appreciate being disturbed after ten o'clock in the evening.

In fact he did not take at all kindly to having his viewing of a basketball game interrupted, but James, professing more interest in and knowledge of the game than he in fact possessed, managed to get himself invited in to view the end of it.

The caretaker then produced beer, James produced banknotes, and a conversation reasonably satisfactory to both of them ensued.

Miss Rosa Leaming, occupant of the top floor apartment in the front of the building, was away for six months. She had sublet it to a friend of a friend, but the deal had fallen through at the last moment, and she had not had time to arrange anything else before departing for New Zealand. The caretaker had promised to keep the flat occupied—not a difficult task owing to the great demand for accommodation in this part of London—and they had come to a suitable financial arrangement.

The managing agents had no objection. He—Jack Sykes—had looked after the place for many years, and they knew they would never get anybody else so trustworthy. The theme of his own worthiness occupied the next few minutes, and James listened politely.

"I suppose the apartment is occupied at the moment, then," he said casually when the caretaker paused to slake his thirst.

"It depends what you mean by occupied," said Jack Sykes, with the air of a man who could say more if he wanted to.

"Is the rent paid?"

"Up to the end of this week. Sunday to Sunday. That's the arrangement."

"I'm thinking of taking it, you see," said James, "just for a week or two. I won't be here very much, but I am going to need somewhere in this part of London that I can come to occasionally."

The caretaker did not find this at all out of the ordinary. In fact it turned out that most of the tenants were well-to-do gentlemen like his present visitor, and sometimes well-dressed ladies, who wanted the apartment for a short let. He gave James another knowledgeable look and seemed to promise some interesting revelations, but James was anxious to get on with the business in hand.

"Would it be possible for me to see the flat now? I take it the tenant is not there at the moment."

No, the gentleman would not be coming back, said the caretaker, but of course it could not be let again till Sunday, and there were several other people wanting it next week, but nobody had actually been promised. . . .

James ignored this invitation to produce more banknotes and

asked for the key. The caretaker, who was, as Paula had said, lame in one leg, did not take much persuading to hand it over; but as James ran upstairs he noticed that the man was coming up slowly behind, to linger on the first landing.

Apparently he was not entirely without a sense of duty, or maybe it was curiosity.

The apartment house was very quiet. James could hear no sound except that of his own footsteps on the worn floor covering. There was something rather sinister about the sight of all these closed doors with their grubby cream paint and the numbers painted on in black. Only when he got to the last flight of stairs did he hear the welcome and reassuring sound of somebody's television. It was the theme music for the ten o'clock news. He had spent longer with the care-taker than he had realised.

But it was worth it. Paula would never have learnt so much, he thought complacently as he put the key into the door of Miss Rosa Leaming's apartment. It would never occur to her to offer bribes. She would not know how.

In size and layout the apartment was very similar to Paula's Hampstead home: one large room with two dormer windows, a tiny bedroom, kitchen and bathroom. But after that, all resemblance ceased. Paula's place was crammed with books—on the shelves, on the desk, and piled up on the tables and on the floor. Sometimes quite a lot of removal work was needed before one could find some-where to sit down, and her untidiness had been getting worse since she had been spending more time at James's apartment.

Eventually, of course, they would buy a house to share. James felt that the last few days had brought this event rather nearer, although Paula herself probably did not yet know it. When it took place, there would have to be a rule that Paula kept her muddles to her own rooms; she herself would be scrupulous about observing this.

Rosa Leaming's apartment looked very empty. Presumably the lady had removed her more treasured personal possessions before leaving her home to the mercy of caretaker-picked tenants. The fur-niture was minimal; there were no books or pictures. It was as imper-sonal as a suite in a third-rate motel.

James walked over to the farther of the two attic windows in the

big room. This would be the one where Paula thought she had seen
somebody watching from behind the curtains when she did her roof
walk.

Pink curtains. Shiny and cheap. James touched them with distaste,
opened the window, and looked out at the short stretch of slates and
the parapet beyond. He did not mind heights, but he very much
disliked the thought of all that dust and grime getting on his clothes.
And if he stayed up here too long, the caretaker would get suspicious.

However, if Paula had done it, so could he, and there was one
thing that really did need checking.

He climbed out without difficulty. The deed would have been done
in daylight, he thought. The fact that Cathy had used the bathroom
in the morning of the day of Mrs. Merton's death proved that. The
medical evidence about the actual time of death had been vague. The
hot tap had been running when the body was found, and this made it
more difficult to establish the time of death.

In daylight, but not so very risky, as Paula had already found out.
The branches of the great plane trees in the square gardens gave a
great deal of cover.

Paula had not—thank God—had to worry about the one thing he
wanted to ascertain. She had found the top sash of Mrs. Merton's
window open wide enough to get a hand over it and pull it down.

How would it be if both sashes were closed, as they might have
been on the morning of the day in question, and as they were now?

James experimented. There was no catch or lock on the window,
and the frames were ill-fitting. It was not very difficult to get a grip
on the upper sash and pull it down a few inches into the position in
which Paula had found it.

James left it that way and retreated. He had had to take the risk
that the room might now be occupied, but fortunately he was not
pursued by any screams of rage or fear.

How about Mrs. Merton? Had she been wide awake and seen a
man climbing through the window? There was not much she could
do about it, poor thing, but she would have recognised him almost
immediately, and been puzzled rather than afraid.

One could imagine the scene.

"What on earth are you doing, Frank? You gave me the fright of my life."

Perhaps a shortage of breath, a pain, a threatened heart attack.

"Sorry, Ma. I'll explain it all. Here, quick. Take some of your pills."

A pause to recover, and then, "Have you talked to her yet, Ma?"

"No. I've tried to, and I'm not going to try again." Sleepy now, but determined. "She's not going to be any good to us. I think we ought to leave it alone. We're very well off as we are."

Something along these lines, the old woman having gone only very reluctantly along with Frank's plan, and not really wanting Cathy to come into their lives at all.

So she had to be snuffed out. A pillow, or maybe she was quite unconscious by now, and the bath-water would finish her off.

James developed the scene in his mind as he returned to Rosa Leaming's apartment. Maybe Mrs. Merton had not received a fright at all; maybe it had been arranged between them beforehand that he should check up on her progress in this way.

James was back in Rosa Leaming's apartment, examining the cooker in the kitchen, when the caretaker appeared, limping more than ever and obviously very sorry for himself and not pleased with James.

There goes another ten-pound note, said James to himself as he explained that he would be wanting to do some cooking and entertaining during his brief tenancy of the flat.

"It doesn't look as if the kitchen has been used recently," he concluded. "Maybe the present tenant didn't want to be bothered."

As he spoke, he opened the door of the fridge; it was completely empty. There was no sign of any eating or drinking having taken place here, not even an empty beer can.

James was about to suggest that the bedroom might perhaps have seen greater use, but decided that the caretaker was not now in a mood to indulge in gossip. In fact, Jack Sykes was looking distinctly suspicious of him. It would be best to conclude the deal and be gone.

"Okay, I'll take it for a week from Sunday," he said briskly. "Here's the rent in advance, plus deposit, and I'll collect the key from you then."

He handed over the key and the cash. Paula, having good reason to know how generous James was, would have noticed that he did not enjoy parting with so much money to the caretaker.

Indeed, James was becoming more and more convinced that Jack Sykes had already received a substantial sum to keep quiet about the present tenant.

If it really was Frank Merton, how much would he have offered? Or would he, perhaps, have some hold over the old man that would serve instead?

As they came downstairs, James debated the possibility of trying to outbid Frank, but finally decided against it. The caretaker must know something more, but there was very little likelihood that it would be conclusive evidence. Even if Frank had been seen on the roof, it still proved nothing. He could claim, with great plausibility, that he wanted to make sure one really could escape that way from a fire.

And if he had been seen actually getting through Mrs. Merton's window? He had locked himself out, of course; he couldn't get back through his own window.

There was no more to be learned here at the moment. Now for Bloomsbury Lodge.

James came up the front doorstep without any clear idea of what he was going to do. Paula seemed to have covered the ground here pretty thoroughly, not to mention the fact that the police had been called in and that a coroner had now pronounced the death to be accidental.

But perhaps there was something fresh to be discovered by a fresh eye and mind going over the ground. He had never been up to the attics, and maybe it would bring him inspiration. At least he would feel he was doing something, and it would stop him from worrying about Paula for a little while.

He got no farther than the front hall.

By the reception desk a harassed-looking grey-haired woman was arguing with an elegant girl wearing a crimson sari. They barely glanced in his direction as he walked purposefully towards the door of the lounge.

Mrs. Gainsborough and the acting girl, thought James. They don't know me, but I know quite a bit about them.

At the back of the hall, near to the lounge door, were a couple of armchairs. James sat down in one of them and looked at his watch as if he were waiting for somebody to keep an appointment. Then he picked up a newspaper and listened.

The argument appeared to concern the girl's veracity. From what James had heard about this, it was probably non-existent, but at this moment she sounded extremely indignant at being doubted.

"I don't believe you," Mrs. Gainsborough was saying. "Why should he come back and then go away again without speaking to anybody?"

"Perhaps he came to fetch his possessions from his room," said the girl. "Perhaps he was afraid that you would treat him badly."

This last remark infuriated Mrs. Gainsborough. "If we did treat him badly, it would be no more than he deserved! Going off and leaving us in the lurch without a receptionist like that! Totally irresponsible, like all young people nowadays."

"But you had me to take over the job," was the calm retort. "And I am a much better reception clerk than that sulky Spanish boy, am I not? I am friendly with people. I make them feel at home. I make them laugh."

That last, at least, is true, said James to himself. She certainly livens this place up.

At this point a third voice was heard. An elderly man had come downstairs and wanted a taxi. James heard Mira deal with this in her most efficient manner and then return to what was presumably her genuine voice, if indeed she possessed such a thing.

"If he has been stealing," she said, "then he would not wish to be seen, would he, Mrs. Gainsborough?"

"If he has been stealing," retorted the other, "then he would not come back here at all. I don't believe you saw him, Mira. And if you did see him, then you ought to have stopped him and come to tell me at once."

"And how should I, who am five feet high, hold on to a great boy who is twice my size?"

James suppressed a laugh. Mrs. Gainsborough made some reply, but she was showing signs of weakening. Keep going, James mentally urged her; keep going until I learn a little more about what has happened. Mira must have said she had seen Carlos come back to Bloomsbury Lodge, but had not seen him leave. That much was plain, and James felt very inclined to believe her.

Marjorie Gainsborough, on the other hand, was determined not to. It would not suit her at all to have Carlos back at Bloomsbury Lodge. The longer he remained missing, the better. And so the argument smouldered on for a little longer, but James learned nothing new, and since he was beginning to find the waiting and listening rather tedious, he decided to take part.

"Excuse me," he said, getting up and approaching the reception desk, "but could either of you tell me whether Professor Helen Mc-Clintock is in residence? I had hoped to meet her here, but perhaps she has left London."

Both women stared at him, speechlessly and rather resentfully, for a moment, and it was Mira who recovered first.

"Professor McClintock returned to Edinburgh yesterday afternoon," she said in her high-class receptionist's voice. "I am sure she will be very sorry to have missed you."

"I am very sorry to have missed her, too," said James. "Just in case she should telephone to ask if there are any messages for her, I wonder if I might leave a note?"

He glanced at Mrs. Gainsborough, but addressed himself primarily to Mira, who responded by instantly producing pencil and paper and indicating that he should sit down at the desk to write. She had not spoken a word, but her gestures were both eloquent and beautiful, and he stored up his impressions to tell Paula.

Marjorie Gainsborough retired, defeated. But perhaps she had merely gone to bring up reinforcements in the form of her husband. There was no time to waste.

James wrote hurriedly, "I want to ask you something. Can we talk privately?" and handed the slip of paper, not folded over, to Mira.

She took it, read it, smiled very sweetly, and said, "In five minutes' time the night porter will come on duty and I am free. Will you wait in the lounge, please?"

James did so. A cheerful televised face was describing tomorrow's weather to an empty room. He switched off the set and thought about what to say to Mira. What did she know, and how was he going to get her to tell him, and what price was she going to ask? Getting involved in Paula's sleuthing could sometimes turn out to be very expensive, especially since he could no longer be bothered to put on a sufficiently charming act to get information free. At one time it had been very important to him to make a favourable impression on people—women mostly, but sometimes men, too. Now it mattered less and less. Perhaps it was the advent of middle age, or perhaps it was Paula's influence, that somehow she had taught him not to care.

What was happening to Paula now? Ought he to be in Oxford, keeping a watch on Dr. Frend's house, instead of chatting up exquisite ladies in crimson saris?

At this moment Mira arrived and turned out, as James had expected, to be extremely businesslike.

She had information to sell. James wanted it, and he looked like someone who had the means to pay for it. A rich man and, what was even more important, a man who had an influential position in the university world.

"All right," he said after a brief bargaining session, "I shall write to the head of the drama department and recommend you very highly. And I will sponsor you for one term. It will be a good investment. You are going to do very well. When you have made your name on the stage, you are going to pay me back. Do you want a written agreement to that effect? I have a lawyer friend whom I can call up even at this time of night."

Mira seemed a little disappointed that it was all arranged so quickly, but that, thought James, could be an act. So, too, were the seductive glances she gave him. He felt almost sure that if she possessed any genuine impulses at all, it was to her own sex that she was attracted, and not to men.

The way she spoke of Carlos rather bore this out.

Yes, she knew him quite well. Yes, of course he was on the make, like herself, but he set about it the wrong way. Stupid boy. First of all thinking he could fascinate a girl who'd got money, and then dabbling in blackmail. He was much too crude to handle that sort of thing.

"Blackmail?" said James, but Mira either didn't know any more or was not talking.

He was not a thief, she said. He did not steal any money or jewellery, but she knew who did.

Here there was a pause for a speculative glance at the questioner: Was he interested in this information as well?

James was not interested in the thefts at Bloomsbury Lodge, considering this to be a matter for Paula's conscience, which seemed to be somewhat underactive in this direction, but he did want to know how Mira had acquired her information.

"My cousin tells me. She cleans upstairs. She sees and hears a lot. But we keep quiet."

"And what are you paid to keep quiet?" asked James.

"We are not paid. We ask nothing. We collect information and wait for a suitable opportunity. Like this one now. With you."

James had the feeling that she was speaking the truth. This one little glimpse of the sort of intrigue that went on behind the shabby exterior of Bloomsbury Lodge was more than enough for him. Paula would be fascinated, but at this moment he simply did not want to know. Let him learn what the girl had to tell about Carlos and then clear out.

Carlos was on duty the day the old lady's body was discovered in the bath. Mira was not in the building, but her cousin was cleaning on that day. She did not see the old lady at all. There had been a DO NOT DISTURB notice on the door, so she had not gone into the room, nor even knocked. But Carlos had been seen going up to the top of the house, and there was no reason for him to go up there at all. He had muttered something about a message for Miss Bradshaw.

This was said with enormous contempt.

It seemed to James, as he carefully put further questions, that Mira genuinely did not know about anybody ever climbing out onto the roof. He did not think it had occurred to either her or her cousin that anybody would ever do such a thing. Every one of us, he thought, even the most subtle and ingenious of persons, is imprisoned within his or her own notions of the world around, and such activity was probably beyond the range of the girl's imagined possibilities. In any case, neither she nor the cousin actually lived in

Bloomsbury Lodge, so even if there ever was a fire drill, which seemed extremely unlikely, they would not be involved.

Neither did Mrs. Merton's death seem to arouse the interest that might have been expected. She was a useless old woman, better dead. What did it matter?

Cathy was quite different. They were very interested in Cathy. Why did a rich American girl stay in this grotty place?

Mira's cousin had tried getting friendly with Cathy, but had not made any progress. That's where Carlos had had the advantage. He was quite good-looking and he spoke like an American, too. Mira's voice took on a slightly transatlantic tone as she said this.

At last they came to his reappearance today, the subject of the argument between Mira and Mrs. Gainsborough.

What time had it been?

Two o'clock. Just after Mira had come on duty. The temporary woman had been on all morning, and Mr. and Mrs. Gainsborough were both out.

Had he come in at the front door?

No, from the basement staircase in the main house. He must have come in through the area entrance. The staff usually came in that way. Kitchen staff, she meant. She, Mira, always used the front entrance.

Did anybody else see him?

Mira didn't think so. He looked very furtive and he also looked very untidy, as if he had been sleeping in his clothes, and that was unusual with him, because he was normally rather smart, in a cheap sort of way, of course.

Had she spoken to him?

No, she had not. She had been very much occupied with a new arrival, a lady doctor from Nigeria, very beautiful, very clever.

Mira's whole body gave the impression of the queenly Nigerian while she was speaking of her.

"Did Carlos go upstairs?" asked James.

"Yes. He has a room on the third floor. It is only a cupboard, really, with a tiny window and hardly space to turn around, but it is good enough for him."

"But you did not see him leave?"

"No." Mira suddenly became less forthcoming. James suspected that she had continued to be very much occupied with the beautiful Nigerian.

"Which is Carlos's room?" he asked. "I'd like to go up and see if he's still there."

"He is not there. Mrs. Gainsborough has looked. But you can have the key if you like."

She got up languidly. She had no more to tell. The interview was at an end, both parties well satisfied with their bargain.

CHAPTER 15

Paula was just about to deliver a well-directed kick when it struck her that she knew that voice. Definitely transatlantic, with a note in it that was a combination of a threat and a plea.

She let herself be manoeuvred out of the grounds and towards a battered-looking black Ford. He could not open the door of it without allowing her to speak, and she said, very quietly, "It's all right, Carlos. I'm not going to run away or attack you."

"Okay. Let's go."

The little car sprang into very noisy life.

"Tell me if you see him following," said the driver.

"Right."

The driving-mirror was cracked and less than efficient. There was no side mirror. Paula twisted round in the front passenger seat so that she could see through the rear window.

"No sign of him yet," she said as they came out into the main road. "It's a Rover, isn't it? Silver-grey."

"That's right."

Cars overtook them, speeding out of the city. Paula's neck began to ache, but she stared intently at the wet road behind them and the oncoming headlights.

"I'm almost sure there's nobody following," she said, "but let's turn right at the next corner and join the bypass road farther on. I know the way. I'll direct you."

To her relief he did not argue, but followed her instructions exactly. They made their way through quiet suburbs and came out onto the London road.

"Keep going," she said. "Unless you'd planned to go somewhere else?"

"I don't know," he replied. "I hadn't figured it out. I hadn't planned this."

He sounded very young and rather bewildered and not at all menacing. Paula began to feel quite guilty. Whatever it was that he had planned, she had obviously upset it completely, and he was now giving the impression of wanting somebody else to take charge.

But she would have to be very careful. She could sense the tension in him.

"Were you running away from the house?" he asked.

"Yes," said Paula after a moment's thought. "I was running away, and I'm very glad that I met you. Otherwise I don't know what I would have done."

"You thought he would kill you, too. Is Cathy there?"

"Yes." Paula thought it safest to say no more. There was a short silence.

"I don't think she knows," said Carlos presently.

Paula made no comment. Fear and shock had subsided, and amazement at this totally unexpected escape was beginning to be swallowed up by intense curiosity.

What was Carlos doing outside Dr. Frend's house? He had certainly not come with the intention of rescuing Paula and driving away immediately. He had obviously come with no goodwill towards Frank, but at the same time he was afraid of him. Had he planted a bomb under Frank's car, which still stood in the roadway? Or fixed it so that the car would crash?

But in that case he would not keep asking if Frank was following, and Paula had the very strong impression that Carlos had only just arrived in Clarendon Place.

"Have you got enough petrol to get to London?" she asked.

"Petrol? Oh, the gas. Sure. We can get to London. Two hours. That's how long it took me to come here."

"You've just come from London?"

"Yup."

"Perhaps we might be able to help each other," said Paula presently. "I'm sorry if I've upset your plans, but I just can't tell you how grateful I am. I hadn't got my car there and didn't know how I was going to get away from the house. I'd like to help you if I possibly can."

He said nothing. He could hardly ask me to help, thought Paula, if his plan was some sort of a booby trap for Frank.

"Are you hungry?" she asked.

"Yes, but I don't think we ought to stop."

"Neither do I. If you can last out, I would suggest that you come to my flat in Hampstead and I'll get you something to eat and make you up a bed, because I think you want some sleep, too."

"I could use some sleep," he admitted.

"That's settled, then. Do you know Hampstead Heath?"

"Yup."

"Make for it, and I'll give you directions when we get nearer."

For a little while they rattled along without speaking. Carlos yawned, and Paula opened her purse, found some cigarettes, and lit one for him.

"Thanks a lot," he said. A moment later he added, "Was he threatening you?"

"Not exactly, but if he thinks I'm a threat to him, then I'm in danger."

Paula hoped this would produce some confidences, but they had travelled several miles farther before he said, "He tried to kill me."

Paula expressed suitable horror. "How did you escape?"

"I'll tell you. Have you got another cigarette?"

He took it with a hand that seemed to be not quite steady, and the little car swerved towards the middle of the road.

"Would you rather wait to tell me until we get back?" suggested Paula, longing to hear his story, but equally longing to get home in safety.

"No. I'll tell you now. I want somebody else to know. If he finds us, and you escape, then you will know what he has done."

"If he finds us," said Paula firmly, "then I am staying with you, whatever happens. But he's not going to find us. He's certainly not following us now, and we are going to my flat, where we are going to lock ourselves in, decide what to do, and telephone to someone for help."

Carlos did not appear to find this very reassuring. "Does he know your address?" he asked.

"Damn. Yes, he does. Cathy will have told him. Maybe it would be better to go to James's place. He doesn't know that address. I've got the key. And we'll be glad of James's help. He's completely trustworthy, Carlos. We need his help. He and I have been trying to find out—trying to find out what really happened."

Paula could still not bring herself to speak Frank's name. She was hoping Carlos would do it first. They were still very wary of each other. It was not so easy to establish trust, driving along in this noisy little car. Paula herself was still feeling rather shocked and shaken, and it seemed to her that the boy was very nearly at the end of his endurance.

It would really be better not to talk until they were safely in James's flat, but Carlos was quite right: If he possessed the vital evidence that could convict Frank of murder or attempted murder, then it was essential that he should hand it on to somebody else at once. Paula had spoken with much more confidence than she really felt when she said that they were now quite safe from Frank.

Had he, or had he not, noticed Carlos's car in Clarendon Place? If not, and there seemed good hope of this, since it had been parked out of sight of the windows and had not been there for long, then they were safe for the time being, because he knew Paula to have no car with her, and he believed Carlos to be dead. But if he had seen them and had followed them, and was choosing the right moment to run them down . . .

It was best not to think of it. Hold on to the fact that Frank and Cathy had been talking in the sitting-room when Paula left the house. It would take them a minute to establish that Paula was no longer there. By which time . . .

Unless somebody had been standing behind the window curtains, peeping out; just as somebody had stood behind the window curtain in the attic flat next to Bloomsbury Lodge.

On the whole Paula was glad when Carlos began to tell his story and diverted her thoughts. She gave him her last cigarette and some fruit-drops that she found in her purse, and he began to talk, jerkily, sometimes almost incoherently, with frequent pauses.

The gist of it was this:

On the morning of the day when the old woman was found dead in the bath, he had gone up to leave a message for Cathy that had come on the telephone.

He knew she was not there because he had seen her go out with an armful of books, but he thought he'd push the note under her door. There was nobody else up there; the cleaning woman was two floors below. In any case, she was a lazy bitch and hardly ever bothered to clean the rooms right up at the top. Everybody knew that.

There was a notice saying DO NOT DISTURB on Mrs. Merton's door. The bathroom door was open, and he pushed the note under the door of Cathy's room and came downstairs.

It was when he was almost at the bottom of the attic stairs that he heard the sound of floor boards creaking. He knew it was not Cathy, and it didn't sound like the old woman; it sounded too heavy for her.

He was rather curious about who it could be. One of the Gainsboroughs maybe, spying on him, or just snooping around, as they both did all the time.

It was possible to keep out of sight round the turn of the attic stairs but still be able to see if anybody walked along the landing. He did this, and he saw legs—a man's legs wearing grey trousers and grey shoes. Very good and expensive shoes. Italian shoes. Very nice style. Carlos had said to himself, I'd like those shoes.

He knew that he would recognise them if he saw them again.

The legs had gone across the landing towards the door of the old woman's room. The door had opened, and the legs disappeared. The door shut.

Carlos waited quite a long time, expecting whoever it was to appear again. It certainly wasn't Joe Gainsborough nor, as far as he knew, anybody else who was either working or living in Bloomsbury Lodge. He supposed it must be somebody visiting the old lady, but he couldn't help wondering if it was someone come to visit Cathy, someone whom Cathy knew. This thought rather upset him.

There was no further sound. Eventually he gave up—he had already been absent from the reception desk for far too long and was going to get a lecture from Mrs. Gainsborough—but he just had to go up again to the top floor. He could not think what had become of the owner of those legs.

Cathy's door was just as he had left it, with the note barely visible in the gap between the door and the floor.

The DO NOT DISTURB notice had been removed from the door of Mrs. Merton's room, and the bathroom door was now shut.

Carlos had come closer, not touching anything, and had looked at the bathroom door. It must be locked, he decided, although the bolt had not been pushed all the way across. Presumably the old woman had come out of her bedroom and was now using the bathroom.

This was what he had told the police: that he had gone upstairs to push the note under Cathy's door and that both the other doors on the landing were shut.

He had not told anybody else about the legs, except and until—

At this stage of the story Paula suspected that Carlos was deviating a little from the strict truth. His clumsy attempts at self-justification could not conceal the fact that he had tried to blackmail Frank when he recognised him as the owner of the legs. Not for any very large sums of money; Paula had the impression that the aim was to be supported while he finished his studies and to remain close to Cathy.

This was after he had driven Cathy to Oxford, at her request. She had told him her whole story, about coming to England to look for her father; if she left anything out, he could easily guess what it was. That night in Oxford, Carlos thought it over. Cathy was ecstatic at finding her father and had no suspicions of him at all. Carlos did not know then exactly what Frank had done, but he knew enough to suspect that he was somehow implicated in the death of the old woman, and he thought Cathy ought to be warned. Maybe Frank himself ought to be warned.

It was Frank who suggested that Carlos should drive him to London. After all, they were both going to Bloomsbury Lodge. It would be silly to take two cars. Carlos had been very glad to have the opportunity of a private talk with Frank.

And Frank, added Paula to herself, had set the scene for Dr. Frend to die when Cathy was alone in the house.

"Where did he try to kill you? And how?" she asked.

Carlos apparently did not know the neighbourhood around Oxford at all. Frank had suggested a pleasanter way to leave the city and join the motorway. He gave directions. Carlos thought it odd that they should be going on such very narrow winding lanes, narrow even for England.

One of them seemed no more than a farm track, and it came to an end by an old shed near the water—maybe it was a boathouse. There was no one about, no house to be seen, and there was water all around—lots of little ponds, or maybe it was a little winding river.

They stopped, and Frank got out of the car, saying they must have gone wrong somewhere. Carlos was beginning to feel very worried. There was certainly something very wrong, and one of the front wheels had got stuck in the mud. He shifted it about, trying to get clear, because he had decided to drive off by himself and leave Frank standing there, but he couldn't get the car to move.

And that was all he remembered.

After that he was sick—sicker than he'd never imagined was possible. And his head seemed to be bursting.

He was lying in bed in a little room quite strange to him. Somebody came in and told him to drink something. After a while he felt less nauseous and he saw it was an old woman. Very ugly, dressed in a dirty old jacket and trousers. There was a younger man, too. Also ugly and dirty. He made the most horrible noises, animal noises, and Carlos thought he was an idiot until he realised that he was deaf and mute. But they seemed to know about looking after people who had been injured, and time passed, and he got better.

Then the old woman began to scold him. It was wicked to take your own life; we must pray to God to forgive you.

On and on and on. Preaching and praying over him.

Carlos thought she was mad, or else he'd gone mad himself from the blow on the head that he must have received. It was almost worse than the sickness. He tried to explain that he didn't know what she was talking about, but she wouldn't listen.

"Did you manage to find out what had really happened?" asked Paula.

"I guess he'd faked a suicide. Knocked me out and fixed up a way to get the gas fumes into the car. That's why I was so nauseous. That's the way they found me. Nearly dead in the car."

"And they didn't tell the police?"

"They didn't like the police. They were some crazy religion that said they must not mix with worldly authority. I didn't get it. Crazy stuff. I was reared a Roman Catholic myself."

"But they saved your life," said Paula.

"Sure they saved my life. I'm grateful. But I had to get away."

That had not been easy. He had very little money, he had no idea where he was, and he couldn't find his car. He suspected that the deaf-mute had taken it. The guy wasn't as daft as he looked, and Carlos could see that he enjoyed being mean to the old woman, who turned out to be his mother.

"But didn't you tell them you'd been attacked?"

"Sure I did. They didn't believe me."

"But that blow on the head."

"Karate, I guess. Anyway, it left no mark. She said I was a wicked sinner to try to take my own life and pretend that somebody else had done it. She said she was going to save me. She asked me where I came from, and when I told her, she tried to get me to talk Spanish. Me speak Spanish! I'm a citizen of the United States of America. I went through college at Lubbock, Texas."

Paula smiled to herself at his indignation, but aloud she spoke soothingly, and he told her a little of his childhood. He really was a poor abandoned illegitimate child, and had made his way to some sort of status and purpose in life by his own efforts alone. That must be why Cathy had been so concerned about him. Some sort of guilt, some sort of fellow feeling. She, too, had been an abandoned illegitimate child, but by no means a poor one, and she had needed to make no effort at all. It all began to make more sense now.

The manner of Carlos's eventual escape occupied the last part of the journey, somewhat interrupted by Paula's instructions as to which road to take.

The deaf-mute had helped him, pleased to be cheating his mother. They had managed to communicate with each other a little, and the man retrieved the car, brought Carlos to some sort of main road, and gave him some chocolate and a little money which, added to what

Carlos already had, came to about five pounds. If he ever found that place again, he'd like to pay it back, and maybe do something for the guy.

His first impulse had been to return to the Oxford house and frighten Frank Merton out of his wits, but wiser counsels prevailed. Frank's motive for murdering him was now overwhelming, and the second attempt would undoubtedly have succeeded.

"But you did go to Oxford," interposed Paula.

"Not till later. I went to London first. I wanted to get something from Bloomsbury Lodge."

Paula thought it quite understandable that he should go to what was, in England, his only home.

"I'd got some more money there," he went on, "but I didn't stay to talk to anybody. I didn't want to be seen."

That, too, was natural enough. But why did he then come to Oxford? Why didn't he go straight to the police and tell them what had happened?

"They wouldn't have believed me," was the simple reply.

Paula did not know what to say to this. She herself certainly believed his story, except for a few places where he had probably glossed over his own actions and motives; but then she knew a great deal about the people involved. It would, perhaps, to somebody who did not know so much, sound a rather fantastic tale to tell about a respectable citizen like Frank Merton, and Carlos was in any case disinclined to trust anybody. Had they not been thrown together in such a dramatic manner, Paula doubted whether he would have trusted her.

The boy sounded as if he had plenty of self-confidence; he was obviously a survivor and determined to fight for survival, but underneath the surface assurance there was a glimpse of something vulnerable and easily hurt.

He was very young. He might turn out well. There were good possibilities in him, but he needed encouragement, and at the moment he wasn't getting very much of it, with the Gainsboroughs trying to pin their thefts on him and Frank trying to murder him. If he got much more of this sort of treatment he could sink back into being the victim, the outcast, at war with society and suspecting everybody.

"You've not been breaking any laws, have you?" asked Paula, trying to make it sound like a joke, and relieved when he did not take offence.

"No, I guess not. Maybe traffic regulations sometimes. I don't understand them here in England."

"Neither do I. And as you say, you are an American citizen. And if necessary you can get somebody to vouch for you. And you have been doing a job—"

Paula broke off. She had spoken without thinking. If anybody was going to give Carlos a good character reference, it was certainly not Joe or Marjorie Gainsborough.

"Though maybe it's best to keep Bloomsbury Lodge out of it," she said. "I'll help you if I can. And maybe Cathy—"

"Cathy does what he tells her."

"Oh no, Carlos. That's not quite true. Of course she is very influenced by him, but she's been very concerned about you, and—"

Again Paula broke off. Perhaps it was better not to mention that fake phone call, since it would add even more fuel to the flames of vengeance.

In any case, they had now reached the pleasant cul-de-sac in which James's apartment block was situated. Carlos looked rather surprised when they came in at the front entrance and he realised that it was quite a superior sort of place. Perhaps he thought that all English academics lived in a Bloomsbury Lodge sort of squalor. Paula persuaded him in, with promises of food and rest and safety, and was rather surprised to find James not at home. But there was no reason he should not have gone out, after he had telephoned Oxford as promised, for there had been nothing more he could have done.

The black cat, Rosie, welcomed her, but sniffed suspiciously at Carlos, who looked uneasy until the examination was over and then bent to stroke her.

"Cathy likes cats," he said.

"I know," said Paula, remembering her first long conversation with the girl. "Poor Cathy. She's got a bad time coming."

"Yeah. It's tough."

But he knows as well as or better than I do what this is going to mean to Cathy, said Paula to herself; there's no need to plead her cause.

Aloud she said, "The bathroom's over there, and I'm going to fix you a meal. Any likes or dislikes? Cold chicken? Tomato soup?"

"That will be fine."

He looked very tired now, very young and vulnerable. Paula made herself coffee and watched him eat. He thanked her several times, but otherwise ate without speaking. Paula had been hoping that James would come in before Carlos went to sleep in the guest-room, but he did not arrive in time, and it was an hour later before she was telling him the whole story.

CHAPTER 16

"Do you think he meant to use this on Frank?" asked Paula, handing over to James the knife that she had found in the pocket of Carlos's windbreaker.

"Wicked-looking thing," said James. "I suppose he picked it up at Bloomsbury Lodge together with the money and a change of clothes. I didn't find anything of interest in his room, but there was a locked drawer in the closet. Private vengeance, do you think? Or as defence?"

"Perhaps a bit of both, but I'd be inclined to say that he was all set to dispose of Frank before Frank disposed of him. I guess I rescued him just as much as he rescued me. So what do we do now, James?"

"We hand it over to the police, of course. As we ought to have done before. We can't handle a fully documented attempted murder."

"Do we have to call them now? I'd hate to wake the boy, and I could do with some sleep myself. So could you."

James felt that they ought to get on with it straight away. After all, here was fresh evidence that would have led to a very different verdict at the inquest on Mrs. Merton, had it been produced at the time. Carlos must tell his full story. With the backing of James and Paula he would be taken seriously. Frank Merton was a public menace and must not remain any longer at large.

But a couple of hours wouldn't make any difference, pleaded Paula. Frank didn't know that his murder attempt on Carlos had failed. All he knew was that Paula had run away. He would be plotting something, no doubt, but he was no immediate threat. No more than he had been yesterday and all the days before.

"I agree that he probably doesn't actually know that Carlos did not die," said James, "but he must have been looking out for some report of the suicide in the local papers. Even in our violence-sodden times it would merit a brief mention. He might even have been back to the place. Aren't murderers supposed to be irresistibly attracted back to the scene of their crime?"

"So it's said, but I don't see how Frank could have done that. He would have found out that Carlos was still alive. He'd have seen the car gone, he'd have tracked down the old woman and the deaf-mute. I'm quite sure he hasn't yet been back there. He would be behaving quite differently."

"I grant you that. Nevertheless, he won't feel quite secure until he has heard an inquest pronounce the death as suicide. And he won't in the least have liked your running away. He's probably been scouring Oxford for you, and he's probably trying to get into your flat at this very moment. And when he doesn't find you, he'll come here."

"But he doesn't know your address."

"It's in the book. And I don't want this business to end in a shoot-out here. The management wouldn't like it at all. In any case, I haven't got a gun."

"You're probably right," said Paula after a little more discussion. "But I don't see that there's any way he could get into this flat. And I'm so terribly tired."

It was now three A.M.

"Just another three hours," she pleaded. "That can't make any difference."

James gave in, much against his own instincts.

The three hours turned into six.

At nine o'clock Paula remarked sleepily that Carlos would now be much more fit for the ordeal of making his statement to the police. "You go and wake him, James, and tell him there'll be breakfast in ten minutes. We'll explain over breakfast what we want him to do."

She almost added, You see, all was well. No murderous Frank Merton, no shoot-outs—but she decided it was more tactful not to say it. James was in an irritable mood, annoyed with himself for having given way last night, still more annoyed at having slept so long.

Paula was in the kitchen, putting plates and knives on the table, when James returned from the guest-room.

"There's no need to set for Carlos," he said in a very cool and offhand way. "He's gone."

Paula dropped a plate. It broke into two pieces, and she stooped to pick them up. "He can't have gone. He must be in the bathroom," she said.

"He is not in the bathroom, nor anywhere else in this flat. And his knife has gone, too. That's my fault," added James in a slightly friendlier manner. "I ought to have locked it away."

Paula said nothing. The coffee percolator finished its task and she poured cups for them both. They drank in silence, standing up.

Then James said, "Don't take it to heart too much. It will save us an awful lot of trouble if he does carry out his own private revenge."

"But he mustn't! I mean, Frank has got to be caught, but that poor boy—"

"It's much more likely that Carlos will be the victim," said James, putting down his cup. "Come on, then. Oxford again."

But Paula was at the telephone. "I'm ringing them. If Frank answers, I'll tell him we *know all.* If it's Cathy . . ."

"Is Dad with you?" Cathy asked before Paula had time to announce herself.

"No. Did he say he would be?"

"He's not been back all night." There was reproach mingled with her anxiety. "Why did you run away, Paula? What's going on? We were terribly worried about you. Dad kept blaming himself. He said you must be nervous of sleeping where Dr. Frend had died, but if you were you ought to have told me."

"I'm sorry, Cathy, but please do listen—"

Cathy would not listen. "I haven't slept all night, and I've been calling and calling your number. Dad insisted on taking the car and going to look for you. I'd have come up to London myself, but he told me not to leave the house in case you turned up."

"I'm terribly sorry," said Paula. "I'm coming to Oxford right away and I'll explain then. But meanwhile this is very important— are you listening, Cathy? I met Carlos outside your house last night as he was coming to attack your father. . . . Yes, it's true." She hurried on through all the exclamations of horror and disbelief at the other end of the line. "You've got to believe this. Your father has done him a grave injury, and he wants revenge. No, not just that fake phone call. Much worse than that. Real serious injury. He's on his way to you now. Keep them apart, Cathy, for God's sake. If Carlos turns up first, get him away, take him somewhere with you, get him to tell you everything, and decide what to do together. If it's your father, then tell him I'm at Bloomsbury Lodge and need to see him there at once. Do your best. We're on the way."

James pulled her away from the telephone.

"Come on. You've done your best, she'll do her best. Let's get there."

"Carlos takes two hours," muttered Paula when they were in James's car.

"Then we'll take one."

Paula shut her eyes and prayed.

She felt so sick and giddy when they pulled up outside the house in Clarendon Place, and so grateful to be still alive, that for a moment she did not take in what James was saying.

"Garage open, no sign of Frank's car. But that's the old banger, isn't it?"

Paula blinked and tried to focus her eyes and her mind.

The little black Ford was parked by the tradesmen's entrance. It occurred to her that the car had covered at least two hundred miles without anything going wrong with it, and she wondered whether Frank had been messing about with it on the fatal day. But there had perhaps been no need. Carlos had said that it got stuck in the mud.

"That's it," she said. "And no Frank, thank God."

"He may have abducted them both at gunpoint," said James as they opened the gate. "Or shot them both and made a dash for it."

"What do we do if he turns up?"

"I don't know," admitted James.

They were now nearly at the church-like porch, and Paula, almost recovered, was slightly ahead.

"We call the police," she said firmly as she reached for the electric bell to the side of the ancient bell-rope.

"Cathy won't want it."

"Oh God, Cathy," said Paula, looking miserably at James.

"Yes, Cathy. The girl with the dream come true. What's happened to it now?"

Paula's fingers stayed near, but did not touch, the bell.

"But we have to do it," said James. "We started this thing."

"I started it," corrected Paula.

"But you didn't cause the two deaths. And you've probably prevented a third."

James reached past her and pressed the bell.

They waited in silent anxiety until the door was opened.

Carlos stood there, unharmed but agitated. "She just won't believe me," he said at once, without any greeting. "Come and tell her it's true." He looked appealingly at Paula. "She says I dreamt it. Or I'm inventing it. But you believe me?" He caught hold of Paula's arm and shook it. "You believe me?"

"Of course we do." James pulled him away. "It's over now, Carlos. We'll hand it all over to the authorities. But first we must speak to Cathy. Be gentle with her. She's going to need all our love and care."

They came into the big sitting-room. Paula did not see the girl at first. The room was so large, and Cathy looked so small, curled up in a corner of the big brown leather settee, her face hidden in her arms, the dark hair limp and lifeless.

Paula came to sit beside her, put out a hand to touch her hair, and softly spoke her name.

"Paula! It's not true! Tell me it's not true!"

"It's true," said Paula with great pity.

For a moment the girl looked all fury and violence, deep blue eyes blazing, hands cramped into claws, a Siamese cat about to spring.

James and Carlos, who had been standing near to the door, moved instinctively nearer.

Then Cathy subsided. "I need more evidence," she muttered. "I need to speak to these people that he"—and there was another little flare-up of fury as she glanced at Carlos—"says took care of him after my father—after my father—"

She got up from the sofa and ran out of the room.

"Watch her, Paula!" cried James.

But Paula needed no urging. She caught up with Cathy two floors up, in the one room in the house into which she had not yet been.

Frank's room. Not as lofty as the great sitting-room downstairs, but that was no disadvantage. Less grandeur, but more comfort. Luxurious comfort—all gorgeous rugs and deep armchairs and a leather-covered desk, and books, loads of books, and every conceivable gadget for music and vision, and pictures . . .

But to Paula it was only a blur. All she wanted was to find Cathy. The girl had certainly come through this door, but she was nowhere to be seen. Paula ran over to the window, looked out, and looked around, puzzled and doubting the evidence of her own eyes.

Then she noticed the white door in the far corner beyond the bay window. A cupboard? No, it didn't look like a cupboard; more likely it led to the bedroom. But it wouldn't open.

"Cathy," said Paula, "do let me in."

There was no reply.

Paula went out onto the landing and tried the main door to the bedroom. That, too, would not open.

"Cathy!" she called out, more urgently now. "Are you all right?"

Still no sound from inside the room.

"She must be in there," muttered Paula to herself. "I know I saw her go in."

Should she call James and Carlos? No. It would only make things more difficult.

"Cathy." This time she spoke with firmness, trying to conceal her own anxiety. "Listen to me. We all want to help you. All three of us. We feel for you very deeply. But you will have to face it. You can't run away."

Paula put her ear to the door. When she had finished speaking, she thought she could hear somebody moving about inside the room.

"Shall I phone Bill Prescott?" she asked.

"No," came a voice from inside the room.

"All right. I won't. But we have got to do something. And we don't want to do it without your consent."

No reaction.

"Where is he, Cathy?"

"If I knew, I wouldn't tell you."

The answer came through quite clearly, and it was at this moment that a new suspicion entered Paula's mind. Cathy did know where her father was because she herself had helped him to escape. Paula's phone call from London had alerted her, and before the rest of them arrived Frank had returned to the house and Cathy had warned him of his danger. What she was now doing was fighting a rearguard action to give him more time to get away. She was horrified and shocked and incredulous, but she was also determined that they should not find him.

"Has he gone to the airport?" asked Paula.

"I don't know."

This was hopeless. Paula decided to give up for the time being and retreat downstairs. At least Cathy had not gone and overdosed herself, and she could not get out of the house without their knowing.

Paula came downstairs to find James and Carlos conferring just inside the sitting-room. They stopped talking and looked at her anxiously.

"She's locked herself into her father's bedroom," said Paula. "She seems to be all right, but she won't come out. I was wondering whether she knows that her father is on the way to South America and is creating a diversion here to give him more time."

"Maybe that's it," began James, but Carlos said firmly, "No. She hasn't helped him get away."

"Why are you so sure?" James asked the question.

"Because she's shocked. She doesn't know what she's doing. When I got here she was crazy. Hysterical. She kept screaming at me: 'What have you done with him? You've killed him!' She tried to scratch my face."

"And what did you say?" asked Paula.

"Me . . . kill him? He tried to kill me!" Carlos lowered his voice to add, "That's what I said to her. Then she said he couldn't have tried to kill me, and what was I getting at. So I told her. She tried to stop her ears, but I made her listen."

James and Paula exchanged glances. They were both thinking the same thing. Neither of them would have coped as well as Carlos had done; it took youth to deal with youth.

"So you're quite sure that she didn't know about her father until you told her?"

"That's right," said the boy. "She didn't know. And now she knows and she doesn't want to know. At least not from me. So I guess we get somebody else to tell her. Somebody she'll have to believe."

"When you came down," said James to Paula, "we'd just decided to seek out the people who rescued Carlos. He thinks he can find the way. Of course, Frank may have meanwhile murdered them, too. We ought to go there, Paula, and take Cathy along with us. Can't you persuade her to come out? Can't you suggest this to her?"

"I doubt if it would help. Maybe Carlos would have more success."

James and Paula both looked at the boy. For a moment he stood at the foot of the stairs, anxious and uncertain. Then he suddenly turned and grinned at them. "Okay. I'll try." And he raced upstairs two steps at a time.

James raised an eyebrow. "A budding romance?"

Paula shook her head. "I doubt it. But they talk the same language. They understand each other."

James looked puzzled. "You mean they are both American?"

"Not only that. It goes much deeper. They're both illegitimate children. Wondering who they are. Crazy mixed-up kids, if you prefer it. Cathy has had a devastating shock. All her romantic dreams have crashed. She's a lost child again. But she's also a furiously angry adult who has been terribly badly let down. She doesn't want care and pity from respectable citizens like us. She wants action. Violent action. If Frank were here and she had a gun she'd probably shoot him. She wants to hit out at Frank. Let her hit out at Carlos instead. He can take it."

James had made no attempt to interrupt this long speech, which Paula uttered not all in a rush, but bit by bit, thinking out her argument as she spoke. When she had finished, he said, "That sounds frightfully subtle, but I think you've got it right. Ought we to melt gracefully away and let them get on with it?"

"Good heavens, no. They'll need our restraining influence. In any case, I want to be in at the finish. Don't you?"

"Need you ask? Nothing would induce me— Good Lord, he's done it!"

Carlos was walking downstairs looking very pleased with himself. "She's coming," he said.

"Did you break in the door?" asked James curiously.

"No," he replied perfectly seriously, "but I said I would if she didn't come out."

Paula's glance at James said clearly, I told you so.

Cathy appeared a few minutes later, looking pale and exhausted but quite calm.

"Okay," she said. "Let's go." She turned to James. "Will you drive us?" It was said in an almost imperious manner.

"Certainly, ma'am," said James.

CHAPTER 17

"There was a gas station," said Carlos, "on the corner. That's it. Turn left here."

James turned, and then sought fresh directions. Apart from these exchanges there was silence in the car. Cathy, sitting behind the driver's seat, leaned back and shut her eyes and appeared to go to sleep. Paula, beside her, was grateful not to have to talk, but to allow the illusion of being safe and protected creep over her, too. James was driving slowly, looking for the way. There was no immediate sense of tension or danger.

Paula looked out at the red and tawny hedges, the ploughed fields, the patches of green pasture, the sudden sprawl of raw redbrick houses, all with the dreamy acceptance of a child pressing its face against the window of a train; noticing details, forgetting them as soon as out of sight. She had shut off her mind to speculation and anxiety. Let the others take over now; let her just observe, but play no part.

Carlos seemed to be in difficulties.

"No. That's not right. I don't remember any church. There wasn't any place at all. Just this one house. And swamps. I guess we've missed a turn somewhere. Maybe we should go back to that little bridge. There was a road just before it."

"It wasn't a road," protested James. "It was hardly even a cart track, and it didn't look as if it was leading anywhere."

"But we aren't going anywhere," said Carlos. "I mean this place was like nowhere. That funny guy—the deaf-mute—knew it, and so did—"

He broke off, presumably deciding that it was best not to mention Frank by name.

But Cathy was taking no notice of him. She was wide awake and looking out of the window.

"It's Wilsham!" she cried. "That's the church. And there's the vicarage, with Virginia creeper all over the porch. It's Wilsham, where my dad used to—"

She stopped suddenly. None of the others spoke.

James turned the car round and pulled in alongside the low stone wall of the graveyard.

"And Mrs. Merton is going to be buried here next week," said Cathy, quite calmly. "Dad fixed it with the vicar."

It was as if they were on no desperate mission at all, but had simply come out of mild curiosity to inspect Frank Merton's home village.

Carlos brought them back to reality. "Maybe we should ask the church people. Maybe they know this swampy place."

"Good idea," said James, and got out of the car.

"I'll take a look, too," said Carlos. "Want to come, Cathy?"

Paula was left alone, looking at the ancient yew-trees in the churchyard and the squat greystone tower of the five-hundred-year-old church. A bell chimed the half hour, sweet and melancholy.

She got out of the car and stood under the lych-gate. A few cars went by; a sturdy old woman, dressed in country tweeds, called imperiously to her dog. A small delivery van stopped at one of the stone cottages the other side of the road. Farther along, past the church and the vicarage, was the row of shops that Cathy had mentioned. Beyond them looked to be a housing estate.

It was a very familiar site: the heart of an old village, church, vicarage, inn, and a few old cottages, surrounded by new developments.

To Paula it meant little. Had she been just driving through she would not have given the place a second glance. But to Cathy it meant so much.

Paula watched her, with the tall boy by her side, walk towards the row of shops.

They stopped, and Cathy seemed to be pointing out something to her companion.

She's showing him where her father used to live, thought Paula, and felt a burst of painful sympathy. But I am out of this now, she told herself. Cathy has a much more suitable audience than myself. A stranger to the place and to the country, who will listen to her with open heart and mind. She doesn't need to watch herself, as she would with me, for fear she is making a mistake about the age of the church or the nature of the architecture or the history of the village. They are strangers together, although it means so much to her.

James emerged from the house with the Virginia creeper round the porch and came towards her.

"The vicar's not there, but his wife knows the place," he said. "And the people. They live a hermit-like existence. Don't encourage visitors. The mother comes to the village shop once a week, never chats to anybody. But the deaf-mute has been known to have a pint at the pub. People chat to him and he grins back. They call him Charlie. The vicar's wife doesn't think that is his real name."

"And how do we get there?"

"It's along that cart track Carlos mentioned." James groaned. "This is going to ruin the car. Where are they? Paula," he added severely, "you've not gone and let her run away?"

"I think she's telling him about her ancestors," said Paula. "They won't be long. It will do her good to talk, and Carlos will listen, but he'll bring her back. That boy is no romantic dreamer. He's got both feet very firmly in the present, and both of them are longing to kick Frank. Thank God he seems to have forgotten about that knife."

"Are you sure?"

"Well, perhaps not. I suppose there's no good asking you to keep out of it if they do have a fight?"

"No good at all. You've had your fun. It's my turn for heroics now. Although I do most sincerely hope there won't be any need for them. Here they come. Cathy does look a bit less anguished. And Carlos is grinning away. He's not a bad lad. On the make, but why not? With the right sort of woman he'll turn out very well."

"Do stop matchmaking, James. It doesn't become you."

Paula got back into the car. Cathy joined her, but did not speak. I've lost her confidence, thought Paula sadly. She's blaming me for all that's come upon her.

"You were right," James was saying to Carlos. "We do have to go along that cart track. I only hope we don't get stuck in the mud. There won't even be room to open the doors and get out and shove. And we'll be lucky if we can get between these hedges at all."

They turned into the narrow track. Both James and Carlos exclaimed in despair as the sharp twigs scratched the sides of the car. Progress was very slow. Paula began to feel impatient with their grieving over the unfeeling metal. "Damn the car," she said, but only to herself.

She glanced at Cathy. She was staring straight ahead now, fixed in her own nightmare. What was she expecting to find? What was she planning to do? Paula still could not quite rid her mind of the notion that Cathy would try to help her father to escape.

The hedges came to an end and they were on a rough stony track, with ditches at either side. Ahead of them were willow trees, through whose yellowing leaves could be seen stretches of sluggish water.

Some backwater of the Isis or one of its tributaries, thought Paula, who did not know the area at all and had only a vague idea of where they were.

"Stop!" yelled Carlos suddenly.

James did so, with a jerk that set them all clinging to their seats.

And then they all of them exclaimed, not in unison, but one after another, as they saw what Carlos had seen, "There's his car!"

The track divided into two. The left-hand branch was wider, but seemed to lead only to the water. The right-hand path led past an old boathouse and continued round a corner between high grass and willow-trees.

The silver-grey Rover had stopped on the left-hand fork.

"That's where I got stuck," said Carlos. "The house is round the corner to the right."

He and James had got out of the car, and James was looking doubtfully at the narrow grassy track.

"I don't know whether," James began, and then hurriedly added, "Hi—come back! We must stick together."

But Carlos had already run past the boathouse and did not turn his head. James, swearing, ran after him.

Paula had expected Cathy to follow them, but instead she walked slowly towards Frank's car and looked inside. Paula wondered whether she had expected somebody to have done with Frank as he had tried to do with Carlos. Or perhaps she was hoping that, cornered, he would choose this way out?

"He's not here," she said.

"No. He must have gone to the house."

"Or that old shed."

"Do you want to go and look?"

They were both speaking now as if they were discussing a temporarily missing household dog or cat, with no greater emotion than a mild anxiety. Perhaps Cathy had had her crisis; perhaps this was how she was going to be from now on, in a sort of cold shock. Yet Paula did not trust her. Nor did she quite trust Carlos, but for different reasons.

The grass track was wider than it had looked at first. Carlos's old Ford could have driven along it. The door of the boathouse was open. Paula looked inside. It was in a better condition than she had expected. The wooden platform was quite firm, and the punt that was moored to it looked old but serviceable.

"There's nobody here," she called out to Cathy. Surely he can't have drowned here, she added to herself.

Perhaps Cathy had the same thought. She came inside and peered into the dark, muddy water.

"We'd better go on to the house," said Paula.

It was a small square stone cottage, unremarkable except for its isolation, and surrounded by a garden entirely given over to vegetables. A few marigolds and Michaelmas daisies round the edges provided the only spots of colour, but it was not neglected. Everything looked in good working order.

The front door stood open. Paula and Cathy walked straight in and turned into the room on the left, whence came the sound of voices.

It was a small parlour, crowded but not cosy.

In a Windsor chair next to the fireplace, in which a coal-fire was laid but not burning, sat an old woman dressed in grey trousers and a dark brown corduroy jacket. As Carlos had said, she was very ugly, and the fact that she was now weeping distractedly made her even more so.

Carlos was crouched beside the chair, trying to comfort her. James, who had been standing by aimlessly, came to the door to greet them and to explain.

"Frank turned up here early this morning," he said, shepherding them out into the passage and speaking in a low voice. "He got in through the kitchen window and came upstairs and into the son's bedroom. They think his intention was—" James paused and glanced at Cathy, who was listening in stony silence. "Anyway," he went on, "the son woke up and gave one of his yells—and this was what saved them. I don't know if you've ever heard the sound a deaf-mute makes when alarmed, but if you don't know he can't speak and are not expecting it . . . well, it's scary, to say the least. They had a bit of a fight and Frank got away and out of the house. The man— Adam's his name—chased him. Frank got into the car and tried to get it moving, but he couldn't shift it at first, and was cursing and struggling away, while Adam, who seems to be very bright, got behind the car and let down the back tyres."

"We didn't notice," murmured Paula.

"When Frank realised what had happened he got out and ran to the boathouse and took the canoe. Adam came back to tell his mother he was going after him—they talk in a sign language—and he would take the dinghy. He knows these waters like the back of his hand. The mother is terrified that he will kill Frank. Or that he has been killed himself."

"There was a punt in the boathouse," said Paula. "Is there any point—"

"I don't think so," said James. "We don't know the waters at all. And a punt isn't easy to manoeuvre. Carlos and I have decided. We were only waiting for you to come. He stays here while we go for the police."

"All right," agreed Paula instantly.

James stepped back into the room. "We're going to fetch help," he said to the old woman.

"He's killed him," she moaned. "It's the vengeance of the Lord."

"Abby, Abby," Carlos chided her. "Nobody has killed him. Adam will soon be back. Hey! I've thought of something. Where's that tea you make? The one you gave me when I was nauseous."

The old woman stopped crying for a moment and showed signs of interest.

"Come on, you two," said James.

But Cathy lagged behind. "I'm staying there."

Paula and James looked at each other.

"I think you ought to come," he said.

"I'd like to stay with Carlos," she said. "Deaf-mutes don't worry me. I told you, Paula. I once taught at a school for the deaf for a short time."

"That's right. You did. Take care, Cathy."

But Cathy had already gone back into the room and they could hear her voice merging with those of the others.

"We'll go back to the vicarage," said James as he turned the car round, with some difficulty. "They'll help us. It's better than going to the nearest phone-box."

"I suppose Frank knows this countryside well," said Paula, "since he was brought up here."

"Yes, but he won't know the backwaters as well as Adam does."

"He could abandon the canoe and get away overland."

"He still wouldn't be a match for Adam on his own terrain. I wonder . . ." James stopped.

"What do you wonder?"

"I wonder whether you're thinking what I am. A deaf-mute, who happens also to be a tough and intelligent character. He wouldn't be easy to cross-examine, if he'd made up his mind not to communicate."

"I am thinking exactly the same," said Paula. "In fact, I'm hoping it. I'm hoping that they will find Frank's dead body in the water and that nobody will ever discover how it got there."

"I'm hoping that, too," said James.

Epilogue

Their hopes were fulfilled. Nobody ever did discover how the body of Frank Merton came to be tangled up in the rushes and water-weeds, near to the capsized canoe.

Adam Farley, speaking through a sign-language interpreter, said that he came across it while he was out fishing in his dinghy. A canoe could be a difficult little craft to handle if you weren't used to it. The water was full of snags—tree roots, rushes, and weeds. You needed to know what you were doing. Strangers seldom came there to fish. That was why he never bothered to lock the boathouse. It was the first time he'd ever had somebody take one of the boats.

The death of Frank Merton was ascribed to accident, a drowning accident, and everybody was very sympathetic towards Cathy.

Paula heard nothing of Cathy for a couple of weeks, and then she sent a message through Carlos to say that she was staying in Oxford for the time being but would have to give up her studies for the rest of the semester as she had so much business to attend to.

Carlos came into Paula's office on his way to Bloomsbury Lodge, and stopped for coffee and a chat.

"What is happening about the Oxford house?" asked Paula.

"Lawyers." Carlos made a face. "Cathy may have some claim on it, but if not she says she'll purchase it. She wants to stay there and maybe turn it into a hotel. She asked me if I'd like to manage it for her."

"And would you?"

"One day. It's possible. Not yet. I want to finish my studies."

"You're doing a sociology degree, aren't you?"

"That's right. I go to night school."

"And what about your job?"

"The committee has asked me to stay on at Bloomsbury Lodge until they appoint a new warden. Longer, if I like."

"I'm glad," said Paula.

She was also glad about the action she herself had taken concerning the Gainsboroughs, which was to tell the chairman of the committee, not the police, what she had found out about them, and leave him to deal with it. Whether or not the couple would be prosecuted, she did not know and no longer cared.

"How is Cathy?" she asked next.

Carlos shrugged.

"What does that mean? Bad, or very bad?"

He made no reply.

"She hasn't forgiven me, has she?" said Paula. "She thinks it's all my fault, her losing her father so soon after she had found him."

Carlos had to admit that this was true. "But it wasn't your fault," he added. "I guess she just can't take it. She knows what he's done, but she has to blame somebody else."

"She's lucky to have you as a friend," said Paula.

"I suppose." He shrugged again.

"But what about you? If you are going to work at Bloomsbury Lodge and go up and down to Oxford to help Cathy with the house, you're going to find it difficult to fit in your academic work. Couldn't Cathy—"

"I'm not going to take any money from Cathy. No way."

"Why?" asked Paula bluntly.

"Because. I love her, but I won't take money from her."

"But you'd have taken money from her father?"

"Yes."

"Just to help with your studies?"

"Right."

"I might be able to do something for you," said Paula, "out of a students' welfare fund that I'm interested in. In fact, I'm on the committee. Would you accept that, Carlos?"

Yes, he would accept that and was very grateful. Paula promised to keep in touch, and they came out of the building, she to make her way to the bus-stop, Carlos to walk across Prince Regent Square.

It was the end of the Merton-Bradshaw mystery, a drifting, uncertain, unsatisfactory end. Paula felt that she could not, in reason and justice, blame herself for Cathy's present unhappiness, and yet she felt one of her black fits of depression coming on.

"Have you been to see Adam Farley and his mother again?" she asked just before they parted.

Carlos nodded. "A couple of times. I'm kind of getting used to them. Abby doesn't preach at me any more, and Adam and I get along fine." He made a few movements with his fingers. "I'm learning the language."

"And what did that mean?"

He laughed. "It meant, literally, it's good not to speak. Silence is best."

"I see." Paula smiled. "Yes, I think we should all follow that advice. Thanks, Carlos. Call in again if you like. I'll be glad to see you. I suppose it's no good my sending any messages to Cathy?"

"Not yet. Some day. She'll see it differently."

That evening, after the worst of Paula's depression had passed away, she said to James, "You've won, darling. This is the last time I get myself mixed up in a murder mystery. It leaves one with such a bitter taste."

"It wasn't your fault," said James firmly. "If it hadn't been for your interference, there would have been a murderer gone free."

"All the same, I don't think I'll ever go investigating again."

"Oh yes you will," said James.

About the Author

Anna Clarke was born in Cape Town and educated in Montreal and Oxford. She holds degrees in economics and English literature and has held a wide variety of jobs, mostly in publishing and university administration. She is the author of eighteen previous novels, including *Cabin 3033, Last Judgment, Soon She Must Die, We the Bereaved,* and *Letter from the Dead,* published by the Crime Club.